To Hanley
Love, Ainslee
Valerie +
Uncle Enid

Tales of a Fifth-Grade
KNIGHT

By Douglas Gibson

STONE ARCH BOOKS
a capstone imprint

Tales of a Fifth-Grade Knight is published by
Stone Arch Books
A Capstone Imprint
1710 Roe Crest Drive
North Mankato, Minnesota 56003
www.capstonepub.com

Text copyright © 2016 by Douglas Gibson

Library of Congress Cataloging-in-Publication Data

Gibson, Douglas, 1969- author.

 Tales of a fifth-grade knight / by Douglas Gibson ; cover illustration by Jez Tuya.

Summary: Isaac Thompson and his friends, Max and Emma, go to Castle Elementary, which is a school in a creepy castle — but when Isaac's little sister Lily goes missing in the basement, things get positively dangerous, because the three friends discover that underground is a world inhabited by a human-sized bat, and an army of spear-wielding rats, and somehow Isaac and his friends must find Lily and get out alive.

ISBN 978-1-4965-0488-3 (library binding) -- ISBN 978-1-62370-255-7 (paper over board) -- ISBN 978-1-4965-2338-9 (ebook pdf) -- ISBN 978-1-62370-585-5 (reflowable epub)

1. Magic--Juvenile fiction. 2. Rescues--Juvenile fiction. 3. Brothers and sisters--Juvenile fiction. 4. Best friends--Juvenile fiction. [1. Magic--Fiction. 2. Rescues--Fiction. 3. Brothers and sisters--Fiction. 4. Best friends--Fiction. 5. Friendship--Fiction.] I. Tuya, Jez, illustrator. II. Title.

 PZ7.1.G52Tal 2015

 [Fic]--dc23

                                 2015000116

Designer: Hilary Wacholz
Design Elements: Shutterstock: Dmitrij Skorobogatov, I_Mak, jörg röse-oberreich, Mad Dog

Illustrations by Jez Tuya

Printed in China.
042015   008866RRDF15

FOR STACEY, ON HER BIRTHDAY

Table of Contents

CHAPTER 1
LILY LOSES HER JEWEL GEM.. 7

CHAPTER 2
INTO THE FURNACE ROOM 17

CHAPTER 3
A LAKE, TWO HANDS, AND A BAT 29

CHAPTER 4
ACROSS THE LAKE 40

CHAPTER 5
THE WELCOMING COMMITTEE 52

CHAPTER 6
RATS, FROGS, AND FIREFLIES 58

CHAPTER 7
DINING WITH AN EAR.. 69

CHAPTER 8
TEAMING UP WITH THE FURNITURE 83

CHAPTER 9

THE PARK 92

CHAPTER 10

THE WRATH OF SHELFLIVER 101

CHAPTER 11

UNDER THE WARDEN'S THUMB 108

CHAPTER 12

MAX SAVES THE DAY... 119

CHAPTER 13

RUNNING FOR THE DOCKS 131

CHAPTER 14

MY LAST STAND.. 137

CHAPTER 15

GETTING OUT OF THERE 148

CHAPTER 1

LILY LOSES HER JEWEL GEM

I guess I should tell you about me. I'm Isaac Thompson, I'm in fifth grade, and — honestly? — I'm nothing special. I like video games, and I get okay grades, and so far neither of my parents has died tragically or gone missing. Until last November, I had led a completely ordinary life. So if you're going to make any sense of what happened to me and my friends Max and Emma and my little sister, Lily, I'm going to have to tell you about our school first. And the first thing you should know about our school is that it's old. It's actually a castle. A millionaire had it brought over from England and put back together at the top of Clinger's Hill, here in Bennetsville, where I live. When he died, he donated the castle to the town, but the townspeople took one look at this creepy, drafty, damp heap of rocks with a dungeon and said, "Hey! Let's turn it into a school." And so our school — Castle Elementary — was born.

Even before the millionaire brought it over from England, this castle was known for weird stuff. It was supposed to have ghosts (including one that turned cakes into pies, another one that turned pies into cakes, and a third that turned mashed potatoes into curly fries). It was also supposed to be cursed (apparently every third person who entered the castle came out in a tutu).

After it became a school, though, things got even weirder. For example, every once in a while during announcements, this creepy voice takes over the intercom and mutters, "flapjacks . . . flapjacks . . . flapjacks." And sometimes all the toilets in the third-floor boys' bathroom turn into fountains and shoot out synchronized jets of red-, white-, and blue-colored water (I've heard that the jets spray in time to "Yankee Doodle," but I've never seen them myself). And just last year, six kids and a teacher got trapped in a secret chamber behind a wall in the cafeteria. They only got out because they managed to tie a note that read, "Help us! We're trapped in a secret chamber behind the wall!" to the leg of a cockroach.

But the weirdest thing that ever happened at our school happened to me and my friends and my little sister. Our story started when the four of us stayed after school with some other kids to rehearse the school play. (Lily wasn't *in* the play, but she stayed after so Mom could pick us up at the same time.)

The play was *The Sword in the Stone*, and in it King Arthur (actually Billy Rodriguez) proves he's king by pulling a sword from an anvil set on top of a stone. (I'm pretty sure that's *not* how you become a king, but it's not like Mrs. Applebaum cares what I think. We go to *Castle* Elementary, and the play had knights and stuff in it, and that was enough for her.) Old Man McTavish, our school janitor, had put together the stone/anvil/sword setup, and nobody could get the sword out. Not Billy Rodriguez, not Mrs. Applebaum. Not my best friend Max — he gave it a try because he's crazy about knights and had wanted to play King Arthur except Mrs. Applebaum said he was too small to be the lead.

Max got it into his head that if he got the sword out they'd *have* to make him King Arthur, so he stood on the anvil and pulled, he laid it on its side and pulled, and he held it upside down (using his feet) and pulled until he got red in the face and Mrs. Applebaum told him to take a rest. But the sword never moved, and finally Mrs. Applebaum sent Billy Rodriguez to get Old Man McTavish, who had to take the whole thing apart.

With all that, the rehearsal went an hour long, and by that time, I had forgotten about Lily. I didn't completely forget — I didn't *leave* without her — but I didn't remember her until everyone was gone, and Mrs. Applebaum had turned out most of the lights and gone out herself, and it was me and Max and Emma inside our big, dark cafeteria that doubles as an auditorium.

"Lily?" My voice echoed. "Lily?"

Emma said we should split up and look for her, so Max looked under all the tables on one side of the cafeteria. I looked under the tables on the other side. And Emma went backstage. We checked and double-checked, but we didn't find Lily until Emma came from backstage and started looking in the storage space *under* the stage.

And that's where Lily was.

She hadn't heard us because she was playing with her ElfSelf dolls. If you're lucky enough not to have heard of ElfSelf dolls, they're these little dolls that look like, well, elves, I guess, with silky wings and pointy ears and hair in different neon colors. I don't know how many of them they make, but each one comes with a piece of a costume — a bracelet, or a ring, or even a kind of a dress — that matches something the elf is wearing but is kid-sized. That's why they call it ElfSelf — you get to put on this costume and pretend you're one of the dolls. (Their jingle ends, "And you can be an elf — yourself! ElfSelf!" I hate that song.)

So Lily was playing with an elf doll that had a crown, and she also wore a crown, a rickety plastic thing with a big red round plastic jewel on the front. And she was completely out of it.

Lily is like that. When she plays, she *plays*, and it can be really hard to get through to her.

I know this is going to sound immature — that's what my mom would call it — but we were already late leaving, and we'd been looking and calling for Lily for ten minutes. She could have answered at any time, and we could've been out of there by then. So to see her there playing with her doll and wearing her crown made me mad. And that's why I reached under the stage, grabbed her arm, and dragged her out of the cafeteria.

"Isaac! Let go of me!" she yelled.

I knew I was being mean, but *honestly*. It was getting late, I was getting hungry, and Lily was getting on my nerves. So I dragged her down the hall toward the parking lot.

And that's when it happened. I heard a loud *clack*, then a sharp *tick tick ticka ticka tick tick tick roll*. Lily screamed even louder for a second, and I turned around.

There on the floor was her ElfSelf crown. I was glad to have an excuse to stop for a moment and calm down, so I took a deep breath, picked up the crown, and tried to hand it to Lily, who was standing with her lips scrunched up and her eyebrows close together. *At least she isn't crying*, I thought. If Mom noticed she was mad, she'd just assume we'd had a fight. If she saw Lily crying, though, I would be in trouble.

"Here," I said, tapping her on her crossed arms with the crown. "Just carry it, okay?"

"Hmph." I didn't think her lips could curl up any more, but they did.

"Come *on*." I unfolded one of her arms and put the crown in her hand. "There," I said. "Can we go now?"

I had just started to walk down the hall again when I heard the last thing I wanted to hear — Lily crying. "The jewel gem!" she screamed. "The jewel gem! It's gone!"

I turned back. "What are you talking about?"

Lily's face had turned bright red. "The jewel gem!" She pointed at the crown.

Max and Emma came up beside us. Max said, "I thought jewels and gems were the same thing." I had always wondered about that, too, but at that moment I saw what Lily was pointing at and realized I had bigger problems.

The red plastic jewel that had been in the front of Lily's crown was missing.

All that *ticka ticka tick tick tick* business must have been that jewel falling out and bouncing somewhere. *Just great*, I thought. Because even crying wasn't the worst thing that could happen. If Mom saw Lily crying, I could always just apologize and say it was a misunderstanding. But if that plastic jewel was missing, Lily would have proof that I'd been mean to her.

I scanned the hallway, saying, "We'll find it. It can't have gone far."

But Emma pointed behind me and said, "I think it went down *there*."

I turned, and for a moment I found it hard to breathe. Emma was pointing at the steps down to the furnace room. Of all the steep, narrow, dark, creepy staircases in the castle we call a school, the steepest, narrowest, darkest, creepiest staircase is the one down to the furnace room, the place that Old Man McTavish uses as his office.

Actually, steep, narrow, dark, and creepy is a good description of Old Man McTavish himself. He's tall and skinny, and although he has a huge bushy beard and a big stringy mop of white hair, his eyes are almost black, and his blue overalls have turned so dark with grime and soot that he sort of blends into the shadows. Needless to say, he's also creepy, and I try to avoid him as much as possible.

But that's where Emma was pointing — down McTavish's staircase, which went on for about thirty steps, and was lit only by a single buzzing, blinking lightbulb at the top.

I gulped, but I knew what I had to do. "Okay, Lily," I said. "Let's go look for it." I took her hand.

We looked for the jewel gem on the first step. It wasn't there.

It wasn't on the second one either.

Steps three through five? Nope.

Six through eleven? Same deal.

On step twelve, there was a splotch of something red. I thought it was the jewel for a second. Then I thought it might be blood. But it turned out it was just a splotch of red paint.

Step thirteen? Nothing.

Ditto for fourteen through thirty.

When we got to the bottom of the steps, we still hadn't found that stupid plastic jewel. We looked around the tiny stretch of floor in front of the door to the furnace room — still no luck. So I looked at the door, and I noticed two things. First, the gap underneath it was just large enough for an ElfSelf jewel gem to roll under. Second, the door wasn't locked. It was *almost* shut, but the latch had jammed against the doorframe. We could go right in, if we wanted to.

I gulped and thought, *Hooray.*

CHAPTER 2

INTO THE FURNACE ROOM

I froze for a second. But Lily had seen that the door was open, too, and apparently we had spent enough time on the steps for her to stop crying and get bossy.

"What are you waiting for?" She put her hands on her hips, her ElfSelf doll dangling from one fist, the crown from the other. "Get in there."

"Don't tell me what to do," I said. "Anyway, we don't know that your dumb gem jewel went in there."

"It's a *jewel gem*." Lily said this as if I were a straight-F student. "And it isn't dumb."

Just then, Emma arrived. "I double-checked upstairs and along the steps," she said. "If it isn't here, then I think it must be in there."

I looked at the door again, took a deep breath, and stepped up to it. I knocked first — for all I knew, Old Man McTavish was in there, and I didn't want to go barging in on him.

No answer.

I knocked again.

"I'm *waiting*," Lily said. At that point, I was about to start dragging her to the parking lot again, but fortunately Emma stepped forward.

"If he catches us, we just have to say we lost something," Emma said. "He can't get mad at us for that." She grabbed the door handle and pulled back. The door didn't move. She grunted, but still the door didn't move. Finally she put all her weight on it, half-falling backward, and the door moved just enough for her to get her hand in and start pushing. Then I helped her push. And finally Max arrived, and he helped push too until the door was open. I looked on the floor, hoping to find the ElfSelf jewel sitting right in front of us, but no luck. It was nowhere to be seen.

Not that we could see very well. It was a big room, lit only by four dull lights dangling from the ceiling and a dim red glow that leaked out of the furnace. And the lights only deepened the shadows cast by a couple dozen huge heaps of something that I couldn't identify at first. As I stepped into the narrow pool of light under the nearest bulb, though, I found out that the heaps were piles of junk. I guessed Old Man McTavish had collected it all, but I couldn't figure out why.

"We should probably —" Emma began.

"I know, I know," I said. "Split up and look for it." Leaving Max to hold the door open, Emma, Lily, and I started searching.

As we went through looking for the jewel, we found piles of broken furniture, piles of old gym equipment (including a stack three feet high of climbing ropes), piles of what looked like scrap parts from old cars, and, weirdly, a pile of about thirty bowling pins, each of them with a face painted on the top.

Some of them were just smiley faces in black paint, some of them were cartoony. But some of them were fancy and colorful like kings and queens from a deck of cards. None of them, thank goodness, looked like Old Man McTavish.

But we didn't find the jewel gem, not even after five minutes of searching.

At that point, Emma said, "What's with these sticks?" and picked up a plain, ordinary stick from a stack of them lying on top of a pile of handheld video games, skateboards, scooters, and a bunch of other stuff McTavish had apparently confiscated from students.

I was about to guess that the sticks were from back when Old Man McTavish kept the school warm by burning wood in a stove when I heard Max shout, "My sword!"

As he rushed to where Emma stood holding the stick, it hit me: wasn't Max supposed to be doing something important? And then I remembered — *the door.* I looked up just in time to see the door swing into the doorframe, and I threw myself at it, but it was too late.

Behind me I heard Lily let out a little scream.

I heard Emma gasp.

I heard Max say, "It's the best stick-sword I ever had!"

I heard Max say, "He took it from me two weeks ago, and I thought I'd never see it again."

And then I heard Max say, "What is everyone staring at?"

Maybe it didn't latch this time either, I thought. I pushed on the door. I rattled the knob. I pushed *and* rattled the knob, and then I kicked it. None of it did any good.

We were locked in.

* * *

Ten minutes later, we were still locked in. We had pounded on the door, and we had shouted for help (Emma had even conducted us to make sure we all shouted at the same time). Then Max tried hitting the door with his stick-sword. After that, Lily tried pouting at it, then crying at it. Unfortunately, though, none of that worked. We were locked in, nobody could hear us shouting, and the lock was the kind that needs a key on each side. (How crazy is that, in a school?)

Finally we all gave up and went and did our own thing. Emma went to stand by the furnace, where it was warmest, Lily and I started looking for the jewel again, and Max got up to look for something in the corner — what, I didn't know, until he gave a shout like he had just won a million dollars, ran into the middle of the room with his hands clasped together, and said, "Guys! I just caught a cockroach! Does anyone have any string or a piece of paper?"

I realized then that Max might have felt a little bad about getting us locked in. But even though we had plenty of pieces of paper, we couldn't find any string anywhere. Eventually Emma pointed out that even if we could tie a note to the cockroach's leg, there might not be anyone outside to read it. So I said, "Max, that was a good idea, but I think we're just going to have to focus on finding the jewel gem."

Max sighed, released the cockroach, and joined Lily and me next to a pile of rusty bicycle wheels.

After a little while, Emma organized another search, with each of us taking part of the room. Max was near the door, Emma took the middle part (which was near the furnace), and Lily and I searched the back. We looked under every pile of junk or stack of confiscated items, but that plastic jewel never turned up. Lily and I were about to look in a pile of junk at one of the rear corners of the room when I heard Max say, "Hey, here's a switch. Maybe it'll turn on some more lights."

Emma had just enough time to say, "Max, all the lights are on already," when everything went as dark as you'd expect for a locked room in the basement of a creepy castle set on a hill.

"Oops, sorry," Max said. "Hey, where's the switch?" We heard his hands slapping the wall. Then he said, "Got it!" and the lights came back on.

I heard Emma give a sigh of relief.

I heard Max giggle softly.

But I didn't hear Lily say anything at all.

"Lily?" I looked around. I couldn't see her. "Lily?" No answer. I called out to Max and Emma, "Do you guys see Lily?"

"Isn't she with you?" Max asked.

"She *was*," I said. I looked behind some piles of junk. Still no Lily.

"Maybe she's hiding," Emma said. "Maybe she wants us to look for her."

"We're already looking for her jewel," I said.

Emma gave me a shrug as if to say, *She's a little kid, what are you going to do?* and came to join me at the back of the room. Max came, too, and for about five minutes we searched and called for Lily, but she was gone.

At that point, Max, who was looking in the corner that Lily and I had been about to search, said, "Hey, look at this."

He pushed away a broken chair. Behind it was a hole in the wall — a tunnel, actually, just big enough for a first grader to crouch through, and just big enough for a fifth grader to crawl through if he had to chase after the first grader.

"Do you think she —" Emma began, but then she stopped as Max picked up something lying just inside the hole. He held it up. It was an ElfSelf elf with shiny pink hair and a crown.

The crown had a red dot painted on the front.

Emma's eyes went wide. "That's —"

I took the doll from Max. "Yep," I said. "That's Lily's."

All three of us shouted down the hole at once: "LILY!"

Nobody answered.

I knelt down and shouted again. My voice echoed through the tunnel, but still nobody answered.

You have got to be kidding, I thought.

"Is she in there?" Max asked, peering into the darkness.

"Where else would she be?" I replied.

"Are you going to go after her?" Emma asked, but it sounded like she didn't think that was a good idea.

Ordinarily I would've agreed with her. If there was ever a point where you should just give up and go get an adult, it was right then. Except any nearby adults were somewhere on the other side of a locked door. And even Emma had admitted that, as far as we knew, none of them would show up to open that door until the next morning. By then, who knew what would happen? At this rate, Lily might be halfway to Mars.

"I don't have any choice," I said, and I started to crawl in.

"Cool," Max said. "I'm going with you."

Emma was *not* happy. "You're going to leave me alone?"

I backed out a little. "The door's locked. What's going to happen? If anything, you'll get rescued first."

"Why does Max have to go?" Emma asked. She started to pout.

"He doesn't *have* to go," I said. "He volunteered."

Max held up his stick-sword and said, "I'm a knight. It would be cowardly not to."

Emma's eyes went wide with disbelief. "You're not a knight. You're not even a knight in the play." (Which was true. For some reason, Max and I were porcupines. Try making *that* costume.) "And for goodness' sake. That's not a sword. It's a *stick*."

Max shrugged. "It's a sword if I say it's a sword."

Emma opened her mouth, but I think she realized she couldn't argue with Max's logic, because all she did was sigh. "Fine," she said. "I'll go with you."

There was a moment's pause. Max and Emma looked at me, and I realized they expected me to lead the way. I wanted to say that Max should go first, since he was the one with the sword. But then I remembered that I was the one who had lost Lily's jewel, and so I crawled into the darkness.

Except that it wasn't all that dark. We still had the light from the furnace room. And when my eyes adjusted, I could make out the rough shapes of the rocks in the wall and floor of the tunnel. And even after the tunnel started to curve a little, it didn't get that dark. If anything, it got lighter. The tunnel got bigger, too, so that after only about three or four minutes of crawling, I could stand up. A little farther on, the tunnel got wide enough that Max and Emma could walk beside me. A little farther, and there was *definitely* light coming from somewhere up ahead. Now we could see each other and see that the walls of the tunnel had become smooth, as if it had been carved through a single enormous rock.

At this point Emma said, "Do you think we should hold hands?"

Honestly? I was about to say *yes* to the holding hands plan when Max said, "*Eww,* gross," and that killed that idea. It didn't matter much anyway, because just as Max said this, I kicked something that clattered along the rocky floor.

"That isn't —" Emma began.

"Yep," I said. I picked the thing up. It was the ElfSelf crown that Lily had been wearing.

Max shrugged and said, "At least we know she's been here."

"But where is here?" Emma asked. Not having any hands to hold, she hugged herself.

"Only one way to find out," I replied as I put the crown in my backpack and started walking again.

I've heard people say they can see "the light at the end of the tunnel" when something bad is almost over. But with this tunnel, finding the light at the end turned out to be just the beginning of our real trouble. About ten steps past where we found the crown, we took one last turn and suddenly found ourselves in a place where the walls ended and the ceiling rose sharply out of sight. We all stopped in our tracks.

I heard Emma take a loud, deep breath that sounded like she'd just turned into a vacuum cleaner.

I heard Max say, "Cool!"

And I didn't say anything. Because now that I saw where the light was coming from, I had a sinking feeling that finding Lily was going to be a lot harder than I'd thought.

CHAPTER 3

A LAKE, TWO HANDS, AND A BAT

Imagine you're at the beach at night, and you see a lighthouse.

No, wait.

Imagine you're at the beach in the middle of the darkest, cloudiest night you can imagine, and you see something in the far, far distance that might be a lighthouse, except that it's out in the middle of the ocean, and it isn't turning. It's just sending out a steady bluish-white light that's strong enough to make your shadow stretch out straight and clear behind you.

Got it? Okay. Now imagine that you're not at the beach. You *thought* you were in your school's basement, but you've just made it to the end of a mysterious tunnel, and you can see little waves rippling along a pebbly beach about ten yards away. Imagine that you can't decide if the water is a pool, or a lake, or a vast underground sea. And imagine that miles away, in the far, far distance, is that maybe-maybe-not lighthouse I just described.

Got that? Good. Because that's what Max, Emma, and I saw.

And here's the question: if that's what you saw, what would you do? Would you just stand there and stare? That's what Emma and I did.

Or would you run toward the water, start jumping up and down, and shout, "Yes! Yes! Yes!" Because that was Max's reaction.

Before we could stop him, he bounded down to the pebbly beach and started going wild. But then he froze and looked to his right at something Emma and I couldn't see because we were still in the tunnel.

He pulled his stick-sword out from his belt loop and shouted, "Die, enormous bat creature!" And then he charged out of sight.

"Max!" Emma ran after him. I did the same. We ran to the beach, turned right — and then stopped.

Because there, about twenty yards away, Max was *floating* in the air, slashing around with his stick and looking really fierce, but still floating. And a little way out in the water, standing in a long boat that was tied to the end of a wooden dock, we saw what could only be described as . . . an enormous bat creature.

I don't know what you would have done in that situation — and you're probably not going to believe what Emma and I did — but we kept running until we reached Max, who was waving his stick and shouting, "Put me down! Put me down!" That's when we realized he wasn't floating, he was *hanging* — from his collar and his belt. And his collar and belt were held by a pair of hands wearing white gloves.

The hands, though? *They* were definitely floating.

Emma and I barely had time to figure this out before a voice came from somewhere behind Max's head, "I'll put you down if you promise not to attack anyone with that stick." The voice surprised me. Instead of sounding deep and frightening or hissy and creepy, it was kind of high, and it cracked when he said the word "promise" like a teenager's does when his voice is changing.

At any rate, Max kept swinging his stick-sword, so Emma jumped in. "Max," she said. He kept swinging. "MAX!"

Max stopped. "What?"

"Whatever-this-is says he'll put you down if you don't attack anyone," she said. "Deal?"

Max frowned. "How do we know we can trust him?"

The invisible teenager sighed. "Because if I wanted to do something other than stop you from hitting people, I could have done it by now."

Still hanging in the air, Max folded his arms. "Like what?"

"I don't know. Thrown you in the water, I guess. Or —" the teenager-voice got a little deeper for a second like he was trying to sound tough, "held you upside down until all the blood rushed to your head and you died."

"Oh," said Max. He made a gesture that I think was a shrug. It was difficult to tell with him hanging like that. "Okay, put me down."

"Right," Invisible Guy said. Then he put Max down, not gently but not roughly either. "Now," he said. He paused while his hands made a series of complicated waving gestures in the air that I realized was him straightening his invisible clothes, or dusting them off, or something. *Why does he care if his clothes are rumpled?* I wondered. I still don't know the answer to that one. "I am Hans," he continued, "and this is Acro." He pointed at the enormous bat creature.

I guess it's time to describe the bat, who actually wasn't enormous. He was only about the size of a grown-up, but he had the face of a bat, with a long nose and jaw to match, and a pair of fangs coming out of his mouth. He also had leathery wings, though they were different from a normal bat's. They didn't seem as wide, and while I think most of a normal bat's fingers are part of its wing, this bat's fingers were close together. So he just seemed to have long, webbed paws. Still, though, he stood on his hind legs, and his clawlike bat feet splayed out over the dock.

Even so — and I don't know how to explain this any better — he looked smart. And *friendly*. He was wearing a baseball cap with a crown on the front. He wore a blue T-shirt (with wide arms to let his wings come out) that said "Acro State Flyers" in white letters, with a drawing of a bat in flight underneath. He was wearing sweatpants. And his webbed paws were holding a long pole at waist height.

When Hans mentioned his name, the bat nodded. Emma, Max, and I all nodded back. We didn't know what else to do. We had never met a bat before.

Mr. Invisible wasn't done, however. "And now, human children, you have a choice." He stopped here to clear his throat — on "choice," his voice had gotten really squeaky. "Do you want to take this boat and go further into the Underground, or do you want to go back?"

"Whoa." This came from Emma. "What's the Underground?"

"Where do you think you are?" Invisible Guy said as the floating hands gestured all around the cave. "Welcome to the Underground!" His voice cracked again, so that kind of ruined the effect I think he was aiming for.

Now I spoke up. "We really don't want to go any farther. We're just looking for my sister, Lily. Have you seen her?"

The hands floated palm up for a moment. I decided Mr. Invisible was making an *I don't know* gesture. "Many pass over to the Underground Town. It is impossible to keep track of them all. And you must choose for yourself whether or not you will go!" He deepened his voice for this part, but I really didn't find it impressive.

"I don't want to get into a boat or anything unless it's going to take me to my sister," I said. "Has she already gone over?"

"Many pass over to the Underground Town," he repeated. The hands moved as if the guy was crossing his arms.

I imagined him looking smug and decided I didn't like him very much.

"So you're not going to tell me?" I asked.

Silence.

What was I supposed to do?

I looked at Max. He shrugged.

I looked at Emma. She bit her lip.

And then I looked at the enormous bat creature. He looked me right in the eye and gave a slow but definite nod. (You're probably wondering why I would take the word of a bat, and all I can tell you is that he looked *that* smart and friendly.)

"Okay," I said. "I'll go."

Invisible Guy held up his hands, palms out. "Not so fast, sport." (Seriously. He called me *sport*. Can you believe it? Where was the evil, echoing laugh? Where were the creepy floating objects? Combined with the squeaky voice and the ham acting, the way this guy talked made it clear he didn't have enough style to carry off invisibility.) "Not so fast. There's a catch. If you all arrived together, you must all cross over together."

Oh no, I thought, and I looked at my friends.

Max bent over and did a fist pump, mouthing, "Yes, yes, yes," so I was sure he was ready to go with me. But Emma shook her head. "Whoa. No. Not going." She held up her hands. "Somebody has to go back and tell everyone where you went."

"All or nothing, missy," said the voice.

Now I was starting to hate the guy. "Can we just talk in private?" I said as I pulled Emma aside. Max came to join us.

"I don't trust the invisible guy," Emma said.

"Yeah," Max said. "He's big on telling people what to do."

I nodded. "I don't trust him either," I said. "But I think we can trust the bat" — I was going to say *creature,* but decided against it — "person. And he's telling me that Lily went . . . wherever we're going." Again, maybe you had to be there, but the bat just seemed trustworthy, like the way you can tell a nice teacher from a mean one just by looking at them.

"I still think someone needs to go back." Emma looked so serious I thought she was about to cry.

But then Max spoke up. "Can I jump in here for a second?" He turned to Emma. "As a knight, I'm kind of an expert on adventures" — Emma rolled her eyes — "and, well, *one,* that all or nothing bit is standard operating procedure. We're not going unless we all go. *Two,* you can't expect places like this to be here all the time, because if they were, we'd already know about it. So if we all go back to tell an adult where Lily is, chances are good that the tunnel will lead nowhere when they finally agree to check it out, which, *three,* could be never, since we'll also tell them we met an invisible guy and a bat in a baseball cap, and they'll probably think we've lost our minds."

Max took a breath. "Bottom line," he said, "if we're going to get Lily back, Isaac has to go right now, and we have to go with him."

For a second, Emma didn't say anything. And then she said, "*Fine*," and stepped up on the dock. Looking proud of himself, Max followed her.

I said to the floating hands, "We're going," and headed for the boat.

"Excellent." The invisible guy followed us along the dock. Again, you might have thought his footsteps would go *thud thud thud* or something else sinister like that, but they went *scuff scuff scuff* instead, like the guy was slouching along. I decided that if I ever turned invisible, I would still remember to be careful about my posture.

The bat person helped Emma, Max, and me get on board (he gave each of us a little bow as he did this), untied the boat, pushed off from the dock, and then started poling us out into the lake. Like I said, the boat was long (about as long as three cars end-to-end), and it must have been heavy, since it was made of wood, had rocks all along the deck, and had a big, fancy carving that stuck up in the front. But the bat didn't seem to have any trouble getting it moving. In fact, the whole time he poled us away from the dock, he just looked bored and slightly sad. (Maybe. It's hard to read a bat's face.) Emma looked scared. Max looked excited. I can't tell you how Floating Hands looked. I don't know how I looked either, but I know how I felt. I was the one who lost the jewel, and I was the one who lost Lily. I was the one who wanted to get in a boat and go look for her. Wherever we were going, if my friends got in trouble, it would be my fault.

CHAPTER 4

ACROSS THE LAKE

For the first part of the journey, neither Emma nor I said much. Emma was too worried, I guess, and I was getting up the courage to ask the bat about Lily. But the bat was busy. He made it seem easy, but it must have been hard work steering the boat through the dark water and around all the big rocks in our way.

I also had trouble finding the courage I needed. With the light ahead of us and the roof of the cavern low overhead, the rocks we passed looked strange and scary. Once I saw a shape in the water to one side and thought it was some kind of monster, like a sea serpent or something. I was about to shout, "There's a monster!" when I realized it was just a rock, though I wasn't completely sure until we'd passed it and I saw it from the lighted side.

A little while later I happened to glance ahead, and for an instant I froze, convinced that the cavern was about to collapse on us. But no, it was just a row of stalactites (the things that hang down from a cave ceiling) that reached down low over the water. But that's how it went for the first hour or so. We had so little light, and on every side things were still so cave-like, that I saw something creepy every time I looked up.

Then the scenery changed. One moment I felt sad and gloomy, and the next I felt mysteriously lighter. I had no idea why until I looked up and realized that the roof over our heads had risen until it was out of sight above us. I looked around and saw that the water spread out, rock-free, as far as I could see on either side. Without the ceiling hanging over us and without the rocks in our way, we had more light. The ripples coming off the boat's sides sparkled, reflecting the bright light in the distance, and so did the wavelets all around us.

After a few minutes, I felt ready to talk to the bat, who had put away his pole and was lying back in the front of the boat with his crazy webbed hands and arms supporting his head. But of course Max started talking first. All along he'd been walking up and down the boat, checking stuff out. Now he started asking questions, which the bat seemed happy enough to answer.

"Why are there rocks in the boat?"

"Ballast."

"What's ballast?"

"What we put in the bottom of the boat to stop it from tipping over."

"Has your boat ever tipped over?"

"Not with me in charge."

"How many people can your boat hold?"

"Enough."

"How did you know to come get us?"

"There's always someone there. It was just our shift."

"Does this boat have a name?"

"Boat Number 19a."

And so on. Eventually, though, Max ran out of questions, and after standing for a few minutes with one foot up on the side of the boat and one hand resting on the stick-sword in his belt loop, he walked to the back of the boat and started talking to Mr. Invisible. "What did you say your name was?"

I heard Mr. Invisible sigh. "Hans."

Max snorted. "*Hans?*"

"I'm sorry. Is there a problem?" Invisible Guy replied.

Max snorted again. "Well, it's just that you're a pair of floating hands, and your name is, well, *Hans*. They sound alike. Don't you think that's funny?"

Emma was also sitting in the stern. She hissed at Max, "*Stop it.*"

"What?" said Max. "I just think it's funny. Hands. Hans. He *is* his name."

I had been watching the bat while Max was talking, and when he said this, the bat give a kind of rolling chirp, and I realized he was laughing. That gave me the courage I needed to talk to him.

"Excuse me," I said, using my best manners. "Do you think you might have seen my sister?"

The bat nodded. "Hans and I took a little girl named Lily over to the Underground Town about a week ago. But that's all I know."

"A week?" *Oh man,* I thought. There was no way that could have been Lily.

The bat must have known what I was thinking because he said, "Time doesn't move the same way in the Underground as in your world. Sometimes it goes faster, sometimes it goes slower."

Okay, then maybe it was *Lily,* I thought. I was about to ask him where I should start looking for her when Emma asked Hans a question — I think to prevent Max from talking about his name again.

"So how does the boat move?" she asked.

It wasn't until then I realized that nobody was doing anything to keep the boat going. The bat had poled us out until our way was clear of rocks but hadn't done anything since the cave had opened up around us. I had been so creeped out by the journey and so worried about Lily that I hadn't even noticed.

At any rate, Hans wasn't interested in answering Emma's question. One of his floating hands jerked a thumb at the bat. "Ask him," he said.

Emma and Max came forward, and we all gathered around the bat. He was still stretched out, and even though he looked weird with his webby wings behind his head, he also looked relaxed, and I think that gave Emma the courage to ask her question again, "How does the boat move?"

"Look in the water," he answered.

We looked down. Even in the dim light, I could see that the water was perfectly clear, except that there was some kind of seaweed waving in it — or I guess *lakeweed*. "So there's a current?" Emma asked. "I can see the plants moving."

The bat smiled, which is a strange thing to see, let me tell you. "The plants *create* the current," he said. "They wave, and they push the water along." The bat yawned and stretched. "They're called rushes, and they make my life a lot easier."

Emma's eyes went wide. "You mean the lake only goes one way?"

"Nope. About twenty yards in that direction" — he pointed to the right of the boat — "the rushes move the water the other way."

Maybe it was the light, or maybe it was knowing that the rushes were doing the work, but when I looked in the water again, the rushes didn't look like seaweed as much as arms or tentacles. I'll say it again: up until that point I had been too scared by the journey and too worried about Lily to fully appreciate how weird this place was. But now, the floating hands, the talking bat, the *things* moving the water — the strangeness finally hit me, and my legs felt weak. I sat down. Right on top of the rocks that were lying there. "Ow." I stood up.

"Careful," said the bat.

Now Max spoke. "What was your name?"

The bat leaned forward. I think he realized more questions were coming.

"My name's Fred. But he" — he gestured toward Hans — "calls me Acro."

Max blurted, "As in *acrobat*?"

"*Stop it*," Emma whispered. She elbowed Max.

But Acro or Fred or whatever-his-name-was gave off that little rolling chirp again. "Yes," he said, "that's right. I am an Acro-Bat."

Even though he was still rubbing his arm from where Emma had elbowed him, Max snorted again. "Of course you're an acrobat. You can *fly*."

Acro shook his head. "Sadly, no. No Acro-Bats can fly." He stood up. "We *can* do this, though."

With that, he bent his knees, jumped to the top of the pole, which was still in its stand, and then jumped up into the air. He went straight up, then tucked and did a couple of somersaults, then extended his wings, glided down in a spiral, did a somersault right above our heads, and totally stuck the landing exactly where he had been standing before.

"WHOA!" Max jumped up. "That was incredible!"

Acro tipped his baseball cap. "We're proud of our skill." He sat down. "But when the elves settled in the Underground, it changed all the ordinary animals who lived here before they arrived. We were common bats, but gradually we became smarter. We also became bigger — too big, in our case. We Acro-Bats can glide, and we can do all sorts of tricks in the air, but we can't actually fly."

"Elves?" Even though I was talking to an enormous intelligent bat in a baseball cap, I was sure he was putting us on. "There are *elves*?"

Acro nodded. "When your kind took over your world," he said, "the elves retreated down here. The Underground Town is where they live."

No wonder Lily crossed over, I thought.

But then Acro leaned in toward us and lowered his voice. "I must warn you that animals aren't the only creatures that change in the Underground. We simply get bigger and smarter, but humans turn, little by little, into *elves*."

Max said, "Whoa."

I didn't say anything, but I felt kind of happy for Lily. After all, I was pretty sure she had always wanted to be an elf, or a fairy, or a rainbow unicorn or something.

Emma must have wanted to become an elf, too, at least a little, because she asked, "Can you change back?"

Even on his bat face, I recognized the look Acro gave Emma then, the kind my dad might have given me if I had asked if I could drive the car or go skydiving or something. "No," he said. "You can't change back. And in the process, you become something else for a while, something neither elf nor human." He nodded toward Hans, whose hands were at that moment floating three feet above the stern doing an air guitar solo. "It's called *weirding*, and I believe it's caused by whatever it is that makes elves elves. Magic, I suppose, or some other power. Hans is about halfway through, and that's where his invisibility comes from. Others have turned into more frightening things. So humans have to get out quickly before they change so much that they wouldn't dare go back home."

When he said this, I thought, *Yikes.*

Max gulped.

Emma said, "That's terrible. Is there anything anyone can do for them?"

Acro stood up, shaking his head. "Don't feel sorry for them. Almost all of them have chosen to go through it, usually after years of study and a long and difficult search for an entrance to the Underground. They do it because elves are immortal, and these people want to live forever."

I was about to say that although Lily did want to be an elf, she didn't want to be an elf permanently, which I knew was true because she also planned to be president someday. But then Acro stepped over, grabbed the pole, and used it to turn the boat a little (apparently the rushes didn't do *all* the work). I decided there was no point in saying anything else. Who knew how long it would take us to find Lily? Or how long it would take us to get back when we did find her?

For that matter, I couldn't even say for sure how long we'd been in that boat. Maybe an hour, but maybe longer. And if time didn't move here like it moved aboveground, what did that mean for everyone at home? Maybe we'd been gone no time at all, and nobody was worried about us yet. Or maybe we'd been gone long enough for our pictures to show up on milk cartons.

And so the rest of our trip across the lake ended up being just as gloomy as the beginning was. Gloomier, even, because now Max seemed down — maybe at the prospect of becoming anything like Hans.

After a while, I noticed that the light ahead had gotten stronger. Our shadows looked pitch-black against the sides of the boat, and the boat, which was white, was almost painful to look at. I was about to ask Acro what was going on when we lurched and started to spin a little, as if someone had just put on the brakes. Acro jumped into action, steadying the boat with the pole.

Then Hans produced a bell from somewhere and started ringing it.

I heard Max say, "Holy cow!"

I heard Emma do her vacuum cleaner gasp again.

And then I saw what they were looking at, and I did my own vacuum cleaner impression.

Because judging by the scene in front of us, we had arrived at the Underground Town.

CHAPTER 5

THE WELCOMING COMMITTEE

As soon as Acro had the boat steady again, he began poling us toward a long dock that jutted out over the water in our direction. I had trouble seeing anything beyond the dock because by now the light had grown so strong that I had to squint to look ahead. After a few seconds, though, I could see that the other end of the dock connected to a wide plank walkway that ran along the base of a high wall, a castle-type wall, made of huge rectangular stones. The wall and the walkway both curved out of sight in either direction, and a big arched gateway (with a sign hung above it reading "Underground Town,

Dock 19") stood open in the part of the wall directly across from the end of the dock.

A tower rose above the gateway, its base built into the wall. It was cone shaped, like a lighthouse, but it was much taller than any lighthouse I'd ever seen. In fact it was as tall as a skyscraper. I had trouble seeing what was at the top — I had to shield my eyes with my hand to look up there, it was so bright — but I finally decided that the tower ended in an enormous glass room or globe. This is where the light came from, but only some of it. As I looked away, blinking the blobs of light out of my eyes, I noticed that there were more towers like this one spaced out along the wall. With all those lights, everything I could see — including a few stalactites that reached down from the cavern ceiling like teeth — seemed bright as day.

But the light coming from the towers wasn't like daylight. As my eyes adjusted, I thought that the wall, the boardwalk, and the dock were covered with ice, but then I realized they just looked that way because the light was white, like a searchlight, or like moonlight. White — and *cold*.

Looking at this scene made me pull my coat closed and fold my arms across my chest. Honestly, as impressive as it all was, it just made me miss the sun.

When we were about twenty feet away from the dock, Acro let the boat coast for a moment and beckoned to the three of us. "One last thing," he said. He looked over his shoulder in Hans's direction, but Hans just kept ringing the bell. "Don't tell anyone you're here to get your sister back."

Great, I thought. Then I asked, "You mean we can't ask anyone for help?"

Acro put his long bat thumb to the end of his snout, which I think meant the same thing as when a human puts a finger to his lips. When he spoke again, his voice was even lower. "Maybe because humans give up so much to come here — their families, friends, sunlight — people here don't talk about leaving. It just isn't done. If you're serious about getting your sister home, you're going to have to be subtle about it."

By now we were within about ten feet of the dock. I was about to ask exactly *how* subtle we had to be when another bell started to ring somewhere ahead of us. Then someone shouted in a harsh, raspy voice, "WELCOMING COMMITTEE,

ATTEN-SHUN! TO THE DOCK, MARCH!" and about ten seconds later, The Next Weird Thing appeared through the doorway in the base of the tower.

It was a platoon of rats.

As we reached the dock and Acro tied the boat up, they marched out — on their hind legs — to greet us. They all wore helmets. They all held spears. They all had swords strapped to belts around their waists. And they were all wearing long tan uniform coats that buttoned high on their necks and didn't look very comfortable. Which might have explained their expressions. It was hard to read Acro's face, but there was no question that these rats all looked mean. And the rat leading them — he had three red and gold stripes sewn on the shoulder of his coat — looked meaner than the rest.

When they got to us, the leader shouted, "WELCOMING COMMITTEE, HALT! RECEEEEIVE VISITORS! HAA!"

All the rats shouted, "HI THERE!" at the top of their lungs. "WELCOME. TO. THE UNDERGROUND TOWN. HAA!" On the "HAA," they lowered their spears and pointed them at the boat. Maybe it was just the spears, but I didn't feel especially welcome.

Still, I thought I should say something. "Um, hello?"

"Hello!" came a chirpy, cheerful female voice. I looked up and down the line of rats, and they all just glared back as if daring me to accuse them of talking in a voice that high and happy.

So I said, "Um, hello?" again, and someone stepped out from behind the rats.

"Hi there! I'm Rhonda!"

You would think that by now I'd be ready for anything, but I still needed a moment to take in Rhonda. She looked like an ordinary — if short — woman, apart from the pink hair, the pointy ears, and the silvery wings on her back. She had on pink lipstick, big pink earrings, a pink shirt, and pink high-heeled shoes. But between her waist and her feet she was, well . . . *insecty*. She had two spindly black legs, and something stuck out behind her legs that it took me a second to recognize.

Max figured it out first. I heard him gasp and say, "Hey! That lady has a lightbulb for a b—" Just in time, Emma clapped a hand over his mouth, but he was right. Because what was sticking out behind Rhonda was the rear end of a firefly.

Fortunately Rhonda didn't seem to notice what Max had said. Instead, her firefly parts blinking, she gushed, "Such charming children! We are so glad to have you here! Come right along! Next stop, the palace!" She beckoned us up to the dock. Even though I would have preferred to talk about Lily right there and then, I was pretty sure that anyone *this* excited to be a tour director was not going to be someone who wanted to talk about leaving town. So I got off the boat, and Acro helped Max and Emma up, while Hans gave us what I think was a sarcastic salute. In a matter of seconds, we walked down the dock, over the boardwalk, through the gateway, and into the town beyond.

CHAPTER 6

RATS, FROGS, AND FIREFLIES

I'm not sure what I expected when we got to the town. I think I had hoped we would walk off the boat, find Lily in about ten seconds, and then head home. I had not expected to find an old cobblestone street. And I definitely hadn't expected the carriage we were going to ride in.

I'm going to leave out all the "the next weird thing was" comments from here on. If I describe something you think is weird, trust me — Max, Emma, and I also thought it was weird. Take this carriage, for example. It had four wheels, but each wheel had half a dozen little handles poking out from its rim. And at each handle, a frog was standing or hanging by its front legs, depending on how far the handle was from the ground. When I say frogs, I mean real, honest-to-goodness frogs — as we walked up to the carriage, I saw one zap a bug out of the air with its tongue — but they wore red uniforms with brass buttons and were pretty big. Standing on their back legs, they came up to about my knee. I wanted to get a closer look at them, but after Rhonda got into the carriage, the rats hustled us in behind her and closed the door.

As she sat down, Rhonda said, "Sergeant Shelfliver, you and your Acro-Rats will accompany us to the palace."

The head rat — apparently his name was Shelfliver (and I figured a name that bad probably explained some of his attitude) — was standing beside the carriage. When he responded, he practically shouted in my ear. "WELCOMING COMMITTEE! FOLLOW CARRIAGE, QUICK MARCH. HAA!" The other rats responded with a loud, "HAA!" of their own.

"Very good," Rhonda chirped. "Drive on."

Since the carriage didn't have a driver or even a horse, I couldn't figure out who Rhonda had said "drive on" to. But then I heard a deep voice shout, "Heave!" and a chorus of deep voices respond, "Ho!"

The carriage began to roll forward, a little jerkily at first, then faster. I looked over the side, and I saw that the *frogs* were powering the carriage. When a frog got to the bottom, he pushed up on his handle using his powerful legs. And then he would ride his handle around the turning wheel until he reached the ground and pushed off again. It didn't look like a fun job.

And then, after a minute or two, Max leaned over to Sergeant Shelfliver, who was quick-marching beside the door to the carriage. Max asked, "Hey, did she call you Acro-Rats?"

Shelfliver replied by beating his right paw against his chest (he was also holding a sword in that paw, so Max had to duck). He shouted, "WE. ARE. ACRO-RATS." Then he added, "HAA!"

At the same time, all the other rats shouted, "HAA!" as well. I wish I had thought to cover my ears. I mean, I got it. Shouting, "HAA" after everything was the rats' way of saying, "Aye, aye," or "Yes, sir," or "You said it, boss," or whatever.

But when they all shouted it at the same time I felt like I was sitting in the middle of a karate lesson. It was loud and confusing and gave you the feeling that you were about to get split like a board. But apparently Max didn't mind it.

"Cool," Max said. "Do you guys do tricks?"

Shelfliver turned to him, his face full of fury, and shouted, "NO, WE DO NOT DO TRICKS! HAA!" As if they had been expecting both the question and the answer, all the other rats shouted, "HAA!" right after Shelfliver.

I think even Max realized he had said the wrong thing. He said, "Okay. Geez. Sorry," and sat back on his seat.

Smiling, Rhonda leaned over to Max and said in a low voice, "Don't worry about them. They're just touchy. You see, back in the day, when the rats heard that the bats were being called Acro-Bats, they got jealous and insisted on being called Acro-Rats. Of course, the bats could do tricks — they used to be able to fly, after all — and the rats couldn't, but the rats didn't care. We had to call them Acro-Rats, they said, or they'd quit, and without them, nothing would get done that needed doing. But calling them

'Acro-Rats,' simply reminds them that they're really nothing special." She winked after saying this and leaned back.

Emma spoke up now. "Rhonda, can I ask you a question?"

"Oh, absolutely, sweetheart!" Rhonda said. Her rear blinked like a strobe light.

This response put Emma off a bit. She forced a smile, though, and asked, "Are you an elf?"

Rhonda giggled. "Almost! Almost!" she said. "I'm a near-elf!" She turned her head to show off one of her elfish ears. "I've had these for quite some time, and soon my firefly parts will go away, and then I'll be an elf at last."

"Right," Emma said, scrunching her eyebrows together. "How long were you a firefly?"

"Oh, years and years. I hated being stuck in that streetlamp, but it's worth it to become an elf!" She looked around excitedly. "Oh! We're in my old neighborhood. And there's Gladys! She used to be my neighbor!"

Rhonda pointed at one of the lampposts that lined the street. Inside the glass case at the top, where the light was coming from, was a woman with a human head, human arms, and human shoulders — and the body of a very large firefly. Rhonda waved at her. Gladys, her human arms crossed, glared back. "Chin up, Gladys!" Rhonda called. "You'll be out before you know it!"

I looked up and down the street. Every lamppost was the same. All of them held a human firefly at the top, and that's how they gave light. Emma looked at me in horror. I think I know how she felt: there was no way immortality could be worth *that*.

We were all quiet for a while as the carriage rolled on. Or at least we were quiet inside the carriage. From outside came the sound of marching rat feet, which turned out to be louder than I would have imagined. And I heard another sound, too, which I finally figured out was singing. Even when I realized this, it took me a while to understand the words, and when I did, I guessed immediately that I was hearing the frogs. Because their song went something like this:

Elves are mean. Rats are, too.
Frogs are green. We're also blue.
Years hopping up at the handle of a wheel,

Years turning 'round between cobblestones and steel,
Long years of waiting till our servitude is through —
Just wait, Elf King, we'll get you!

There was more like this, telling the story of how the frogs had been lured to the Underground Town by promises of food, and how they had then been forced to work pushing carriages and serving as exterminators until they got sick. And every verse ended with some kind of threat to the Elf King. I waited for Rhonda (who seemed happy about becoming an elf) to say something, or for Shelfliver to tell the frogs to shut up. But neither of them did anything about it. Maybe they figured it was better for the frogs to get it out of their systems.

By now, you're probably wondering how the actual town looked. But the town is hard to describe, partly because the light made everything look so weird. All around the town, those towers with their glass globes gave off that nearly blinding cold white light. It was like having the moon on every street corner.

And anywhere the light from the globes couldn't reach, you had the firefly-lady lampposts. So there were hardly any shadows anywhere — just stretches of frozen-looking cobblestones and buildings alternating with alleys and side streets and sheds bathed in a greenish-yellow glow.

The buildings seemed to be about what you might expect from an elf town. Some were square, like normal buildings, but some were round, and some were just sort of chunky, with a bunch of sides that barely seemed to fit together.

Some of the buildings stood up straight, some leaned to one side or the other. Some of the buildings had normal slanting roofs, and some of them had flat roofs. Some of them had pointy roofs, or roofs shaped like the tops of mushrooms. And some of the roofs had antlers on them, or antennae like an insect's.

But the buildings all had one thing in common: they didn't have windows or doors. They had holes for windows — some rectangular, some round, some triangular (they looked to me like Halloween pumpkin eyes) — but the holes didn't have any glass or screens in them. They had doorways, but the doorways didn't have any doors. All you saw were these gaping black holes — nobody had a light on inside, as far as I could tell — and so the whole place had a ghost town-y feel to it.

And it was practically deserted. Apart from Rhonda, the rats, the frogs, and the firefly ladies (who I tried pretty hard not to look at), we barely saw anyone on our way to the palace. Only about a dozen people, actually, and these were janitors of some kind, sweeping the streets. Except they didn't have brooms . . . they basically *were* brooms. I couldn't figure it out at first, but then we passed right by one of those janitors, and I saw that he had brooms — long brooms like Old Man McTavish uses to sweep the halls, but a little narrower — for *feet*. I looked up at the rest of the guy. He wore a three-piece suit, and he looked like he should be in a bank or something instead of sweeping the streets. And he looked sad to see us, as if maybe he had kids that he had left behind to come down here.

But then the streets and buildings ended, and we entered a park. The park had wide paths broken up by trees twisted out of what looked like copper wire, trees with metal leaves. And there were paper flowers coming out of the dirt around the bottoms of the trees. Just like the town, though, the park was deserted. So I asked Rhonda where all the people were who lived there.

Rhonda grinned. "They're in the palace. It's dinnertime, and everyone's there."

"Everyone?" *Including Lily?* I wondered.

"Everyone who is anyone," Rhonda said, smoothing her pink hair back behind her pointy ear.

Just then, one of the frogs yelled, "Brake!" and we coasted to a stop at the bottom of a set of wide, shallow steps . . . or almost to a stop. We had enough momentum at the end to hit the bottom step hard — and for Rhonda to fall out of her seat. Again, though, she didn't seem to mind. She picked herself up, swept back her pink hair, and climbed out of the carriage. As I followed her, I looked at the frogs. I wasn't sure — frog faces are even harder to read than bats' — but I could swear they were smirking.

"Come along!" Rhonda called. She was already five stairs above us, her behind flashing with every step she climbed. "We're late!"

That's when I got my first good look at the palace. And honestly? It wasn't anything special. I mean, it was *okay*. It looked like a big, fancy house, five or six stories tall, with round towerlike things in each corner and doorways and window frames that looked like they were made of gold, or at least painted with gold paint. But it was also kind of ugly. It was strung with multicolored lights, as if it was Christmas, but a lot of the bulbs had burned out, so they made the place look more sad than cheerful, like a department store Santa's castle shoved into storage. Combined with what I'd heard from the frogs and the deserted look of the rest of the place, the palace kind of spooked me. I wasn't sure I wanted to go in there.

By this time, Max and Emma had gotten out of the carriage, too. Thinking we ought to change things up a little, I bowed to Emma, gestured up the steps, and said, "Ladies first."

But she'd gotten a good look at the palace, and she gave me a glare that said, *You've got to be kidding.* So I sighed and went first again, which I guess was fair. After all, it was *my* sister we were looking for.

CHAPTER 7

DINING WITH AN EAR

I climbed the stairs to the palace, passed a couple of Acro-Rats (who glared at me, but didn't say or do anything), and entered the main door. I could see Rhonda heading through another door directly ahead of me — into what looked like a hotel banquet room — so I hurried after her, and Max and Emma jogged along behind.

At the doorway, I stopped, hoping I would be able to see Lily, but what I saw actually made me forget about Lily for a while.

I heard Max say, "Whoa."

I heard Emma say, "Ohhhh." And then, "Do you think all these people *want* to be elves?"

Because we were looking at a banquet room full of people. I mean, I guess they were people, but they were also all *weirded*.

There were people with the heads of animals — from where I stood, I could see a donkey, a koala bear, and a wild-eyed chicken who kept pecking at her neighbors' plates and getting shouted at for it. There were people with blue hair and green hair, pink hair and purple hair. There were people with the bottoms of bees, the bottoms of ants, and the bottoms of what I think were pigeons. There were people who appeared to be carved out of stone, or out of wood, or out of sponges. There were people, too, who looked like objects — on the other side of the room I saw a spoon with arms and legs, and, passing right in front of us, carrying a tray, I saw a waiter who I could swear was just the outline of a person . . . in salted pretzel.

There were people in pretty much every possible weird condition, and we stood there frozen for a moment. Then we heard Rhonda call, "Yoo-hoo! Over here!" from about three tables away. We went over, dodging a few more people along the way, including the strangest person I saw there, someone who was made up of three blocks stacked one over the other and a normal human head (with pointy ears) painted on top. The blocks had a different outfit on each side, and they turned as he moved, so he was like a walking mix-and-match book. Just as we walked past him, the outfits lined up correctly, and he giggled and said, "A match! A match!"

When we reached Rhonda, she gave us a big grin and fluttered her hands at the chairs next to her. Her rear light blinked frantically. "Take a seat!" she said. "The Elf King is about to give the toast!"

Max and Emma took the chairs on either side of me, but I kept standing for a moment, scanning the room for Lily, or anyone who might have been her before she started weirding. After a second or two, though, Max grabbed my arm and pulled me down into my chair.

"Stop it," I said. "I'm looking for —"

Max put his finger to his lips and nodded across the table.

Sitting there was a gigantic ear.

But it wasn't just an ear. Apparently it had legs and feet, too, because it was holding a napkin with the toes of one foot — and the other foot was holding a glass of water. As Max and I watched, the ear brought the glass up to its ear canal, poured in the water (it didn't have the best aim), and then wiped itself off with the napkin.

Rhonda, who was sitting on the other side of Emma, flashed the ear a smile. "Oh, hello, Ear-with-Legs! I didn't see you there!" (How she missed him, I don't know.) In return, the ear made a sort of bow and waved the foot holding the napkin.

"Ear-with-Legs?" Emma asked. She looked puzzled. "Has that always been its name?"

Rhonda lowered her voice. "*His* name, darling, his name. He's a *he*. And I don't think that's his original name, but a long time has passed since he's been able to speak. We've all forgotten his name by now — even him. 'Ear-with-Legs' just seemed to fit."

Before Emma had time to ask any more questions, someone began tapping on a glass. And soon everyone was doing it, including Ear-with-Legs, who used his toes for this, too.

"Oh, wonderful!" Rhonda was ecstatic. "Now you'll get to hear the Elf King speak!"

Rhonda pointed toward the front of the hall, where I could see a raised platform. On that platform stood a dozen more round tables like ours. Behind these tables, another platform rose even higher. On that platform, twenty people sat behind another table, which was long and rectangular instead of round.

The people at the lower table all looked like they had come straight out of the ElfSelf catalogue, pretty much like Rhonda would look as soon as she lost her firefly parts.

The elves on the upper platform, though, looked very different. They had the same wings and pointy ears as the people sitting in front of them, but otherwise they looked human, with regular human hair and skin. But they stood out by being good-looking. So good-looking, in fact, that they could have been fashion models. And the two best-looking elves, a man and a woman, sat in the middle of the long table. They wore crowns, they sat in fancy chairs, and they just seemed to have a sort of glow about them. It struck me at that point that this banquet hall felt a lot like my school cafeteria, with the cool kids all at their own table, the slightly-less-cool kids sitting close by, and everyone else sitting wherever they could find a seat.

While I was thinking this, the man in the tall chair stood and held up his hand. The glass-banging stopped.

So that's the Elf King, I thought. There seemed to be something familiar about him, and I tried to figure out what it was, but soon the question was driven out of my mind.

Because right at that moment, the Elf King opened his mouth. He raised a glass as if he was about to give a toast. And then . . .

"BUUUUUUUUUUUUUUUUUUUUUUUURP!"

He burped.

It was a good burp. If ever there was a burp fit for a king . . . that was it. It seemed to go on for about five minutes, with people *oooh*ing and *ahh*ing the whole time. But after it was over, he just sat down, and everyone burst into applause. Apparently that was his entire speech.

Max clapped as hard as anyone. "Again! Again!" he shouted. "More speech!"

Rhonda flashed him a smile. "Wasn't it *wonderful?*"

Max smiled right back. "Yeah! It was the greatest! Woo-hoo!"

I elbowed him in the arm to get him to stop.

After the applause died down, everyone started eating again. A waitress, who looked pretty much normal except that she had feathers on her head instead of hair, brought empty plates and put them down in front of the three of us, Rhonda, and the Ear. Rhonda tapped her plate three times with her knife, and suddenly a full dinner appeared — a steak, a baked potato, and green beans. Across the table, the Ear picked up a spoon with his toes and tapped his plate. It turned into a bowl of tomato soup.

As Max and I watched, both Rhonda and the Ear started eating. Rhonda picked up her steak with both hands and began chewing on it like a squirrel gnawing a nut, all the while making these grumbling, growling noises. And Mr. Ear calmly raised spoonful after spoonful of tomato soup to his ear canal and ladled them in, mopping up the spills with his napkin — though after a while the napkin became so soaked with orange liquid that it didn't do much good.

I looked down at my plate and considered tapping it with a fork or something, but sitting there watching Rhonda the Blinking Squirrel and the Soup Monster had kind of made me lose my appetite.

That's when Emma, who had been staring up at the high table, nudged me with her elbow.

"What?" I said.

She put her finger on her lips and jerked her head toward the front of the room.

I shrugged. Emma gave me a look like I was the dumbest person she'd ever met and mouthed the words "the crown" at me.

I looked again at the Elf King. I looked at his crown. And then I realized what made him seem so familiar.

His crown was gold and kind of thin and pointy, and it had a red jewel set in the front. It was exactly like Lily's ElfSelf crown!

My jaw dropped. But Emma sprang into action. Like she was some kind of private detective, she casually said to Rhonda, "Boy, that crown on the Elf King sure does look familiar."

Okay, maybe Emma wasn't completely natural, but Rhonda, who had moved on to gnawing her baked potato, didn't seem to notice.

"Well, there are a lot of imitations floating around," Rhonda said. "I hear they're quite popular where you're from. Just last week, we had a girl in here from entrance nineteen who thought it was actually hers!"

It was a good thing I wasn't eating at that point, because if I had been I probably would have choked. *We* had come in entrance nineteen!

I stared at Emma, but she didn't even look at me before continuing. "Huh. How interesting!" she said. "Tell me what happened."

Maybe it was because she was eating, but Rhonda seemed a lot less sweet and cheery than she had before. "When the girl saw the Elf King, she ran right up to the high table, if you can believe it, and she demanded the Elf King give his crown 'back' to her. What a commotion!"

Emma clicked her tongue sympathetically. "And then what happened?" she asked.

"Well, the king doesn't talk to just anyone. The rats whisked her away —" Rhonda made a waving motion with her hand, and clumps of potato sprayed across the table "— and took her to the dungeons, and I hope she stays there for a very long time. Little brat."

I think Rhonda noticed Emma flinching at that last part, because she swallowed quickly, put on another big smile, and said, "Not at all like you sweet little children."

"No, of course not," Emma said, and grinned like a vampire about to go for Rhonda's neck. But Rhonda turned back to her plate.

Emma looked at me with a wide-eyed, did-you-hear-that kind of expression, and I felt my insides grow cold. I had no doubt that Rhonda had just described Lily. She was a little girl. She had gotten here a week ago. She had come in through entrance nineteen. She had arrived at a palace, and, right off the bat, demanded the king give her his crown. Who else could it be?

We needed to plan. And I was pretty sure I didn't want Rhonda around when we did that. Fortunately, we weren't there for much longer.

After she finished gnawing, Rhonda tapped her plate again to produce a slice of cheesecake. But before she started eating, she turned to us. "You three must be tired," she said. "Why don't you go to bed? Ear-with-Legs!"

The Ear, who was pouring water over himself to rinse off the soup, stopped and did another little bow.

"I'm afraid I've got something for you to do," Rhonda said. "Could you escort these lovely children to one of the guest rooms?"

The Ear stood up, bowed again to Rhonda, and then bowed to us. Then he started walking out of the banquet hall.

Rhonda stopped gnawing her cheesecake long enough to blow us kisses, calling out, "Sweet dreams!" Her rear light lit up until it was brighter than I'd ever seen it, which I took as a sign that she was happy to get rid of us. And given the way Max, Emma, and I jumped out of our seats, she could probably tell the feeling was mutual.

The walking ear led us out of the banquet hall, and at the doors, a couple of Acro-Rats fell in behind us. As we walked, Emma had a quick, whispered conversation with Max, who had been too busy staring at all the weirded people to hear Rhonda talk. She explained about the crown and Lily's probable location.

When he heard the news, he pulled out his stick-sword and waved it around. "Great!" Max said. "We'll fight our way to the dungeons and then fight our way back out!"

"Shh. No." Emma's eyes darted toward the rats who were following us, but they seemed not to have noticed anything. Before she could explain her plan, though, Max had a new one.

"We're going to fight our way to the Elf King, hold him hostage, and demand that they release Lily!"

"NO!" Emma's eyes went wide as she realized how loudly she had spoken.

By this point, it was finally registering with Max that Emma was hoping for a little secrecy. He said, a little less loudly, "We're going to rent an apartment next door and tunnel into the dungeons from there?"

"No!" Emma hissed. "Acro said to be subtle, remember? We're going to find out where the dungeons are. And then we'll think of something. Until then, we play it cool."

While Max and Emma were having this argument, I was looking around at the palace. Just like the outside, the inside of the place was a little disappointing. The banquet room had looked like it came from your average hotel, and the main hall didn't fit my idea of a palace either. The walls were painted white with what even I could tell was bad art hanging on them. The floor was supposed to be marble, but I think it was those thin stick-on marble tiles you can buy at the hardware store. When we got to the staircase, it was the same deal, with a rickety-looking chrome handrail running along the side and worn industrial carpet running up the middle. *Some palace*, I thought. Rats included, it reminded me of the hotel in Indianapolis where my Uncle Jimmy got married. Except that Uncle Jimmy's wedding didn't have any giant walking ears.

Soon Ear-with-Legs turned off of the staircase, and we followed him into a long, dim hallway with torches flickering on the stone walls — much more like what I would have imagined for a palace or a castle. Ear stopped about halfway down, bowed deeply, and pointed his foot at a door made of thick wood that was painted gold.

"We should go in there?" I asked. Ear-with-Legs bowed again. Honestly, having to communicate via sign language with an enormous ear was starting to creep me out.

"Great," Emma said. "Thanks!"

She was about to open the door when one of the rats shouted, "I'LL GET IT!" shoved Emma aside, opened the door, and gestured us in with his spear. Looking through the doorway, I got a glimpse of what just looked like a normal room lit by candles, with white walls, a wooden floor, a coffee table, a bed, and other furniture. I stepped forward.

"We'll go in," I said. "You don't have to push us around." The rat stepped back a bit, but as soon as Emma, Max, and I went into the room, he slammed the door behind us.

He and the other Acro-Rat shouted, "HAA!" on the other side, as if snapping to attention — but there was no other sound. No feet marching away. They were staying right where they were, and they were guarding the door.

Great, I thought. *How are we going to find Lily now?*

CHAPTER 8

TEAMING UP WITH THE FURNITURE

After we recovered from the shock of having the door slam in our faces, Emma put her finger to her lips and pointed at the keyhole. I waved at her to go ahead, and she knelt down to look through the hole for about two minutes. Then she stood and beckoned to me.

I didn't see anything at first — just a torch burning on the opposite wall — until a big round shadow passed in front of the torch, and I realized that Ear-with-Legs was out there, too. Then Max tapped me on the shoulder for his turn, and I sat next to Emma with my back to the door. After a minute, Max slumped down beside me. None of us spoke as we stared out at the room. It was exactly like the room we'd looked into a moment ago, except that it seemed dimmer and smaller now that we were trapped in it.

"I don't like this," Emma finally whispered. "Why are they guarding us?"

"I don't know," I said. "They just like to be bossy?"

Emma frowned. "But that's not the only weird thing."

"Yeah," I said. "There's also the giant ear, a bunch of rats, and a king who should maybe drink less soda."

"I didn't mean that," Emma said. "Isn't it weird that the king's crown looks so much like Lily's crown? And it sounded like Rhonda knew that, too."

Now that Emma had brought it up, it did seem weird.

But I had more important things to think about. And once again, I was worried about time. We'd been a couple hours on the boat, and taken another hour to wind up here, and we weren't much closer to finding Lily.

"Look," I said. "We came here to find my sister, and I think we should focus on that. So how are we going to get out of this room and start looking for her?"

"We could just walk out," Max said as he got up.

"Max —" Emma began, but before she could stop him, Max had turned the knob and pushed open the door. In a loud voice he said, "Think I'll just go for a stroll. Don't wait up for me." He took a step into the hall — and then stepped back quickly as the door slammed in his face.

From the other side of the door, one of the rats shouted, "WE WILL BRING YOU A STROLL! HAA!" There was an answering, "HAA!" from the other rat, and then silence.

Max sat down next to us, rubbing his foot where the door had hit it. He muttered, "How are they going to bring me a stroll?"

Now we were definitely trapped, and we all sat quietly for a minute or two, pondering our situation. But I didn't sit there long before I decided that I couldn't stay in that room much longer. And not because I was worried about Lily or about how much time had passed.

Apparently Max felt the same way. "Phew-wee!" He stopped rubbing his foot and waved his hand in front of his face.

Emma pinched her nose shut. "Wait," she said. "You guys smell that, too?"

The room smelled bad. With every breath, I took in a lungful of some weird, but kind of familiar, odor. It was musky and outdoorsy and just barely on the wrong side of stinking. But it was enough on the wrong side that I didn't want to breathe, and I couldn't ignore it any longer.

I said, "Why does it stink in here?"

In response, a voice — one that reminded me of some of the cafeteria ladies at school — said, "Hmph. I don't think humans smell all that nice either. You walk into a room, and anyone with a nose can just *smell* all that junk food you eat."

I couldn't figure out where the voice had come from, so my mind ticked through the possibilities. Invisible teenager wearing white gloves? Nope. Firefly lady hiding behind giant rats? Nope. I only saw a coffee table, a couple of armchairs, a few footstools, and a bed. Except for the table, they were all upholstered in fur, which was weird. I was stumped about where the voice was coming from until Max jumped up, shouted, "Die enormous ferret creature!" and drew his sword.

Oh, no, I thought. It wasn't clear what was happening, but I was pretty sure that *attacking* something would not qualify as "playing it cool."

Before Max could rush across the room, though, Emma threw herself forward and grabbed his pants leg. "Why are you attacking the bed?" she shouted.

I looked at the bed, and then I realized what Max had been attacking. A split second later, Emma gasped, and I figured she had seen it, too.

The bed was actually an enormous ferret, all tied up with rope so that she could barely move an inch.

"Well, I guess that explains the smell," Emma said. Then her eyes widened, and she said, "Oops. Sorry."

"It's all right, pumpkin," said the ferret. "I've heard it all before."

By this time I had crossed over to the ferret and crouched down by her head. "Why are you tied up like this?" I asked.

"I'm being a bed," she said. "What does it look like I'm doing?"

"Okay," I said. "But *why* are you being a bed?"

"Because that's how elves make their fanciest furniture. Right, folks?"

A chorus of answers erupted from all around the room.

"Yep!"

"That's right!"

"Indubitably."

I looked at my friends, unable to believe it.

"Oh, no," Emma said.

"Wow," said Max.

What I said was, "Could this place get any weirder?" Because every single piece of furniture in the room — the chairs, the table, and the footstools — turned out to be an animal tied down with rope. The armchairs were squirrels. The stools were mice. And the round coffee table in the middle of the room turned out to be a big glass circle glued onto the shell of a turtle.

Emma's eyes went wide with horror. She held a hand up to her mouth and said, "I don't even want to *see* the bathroom."

The ferret twisted a little in her ropes. "That makes two of us, sweetheart."

I decided to move the conversation along. "How did you get here? How did they get you to do this?"

"Simple." The ferret sighed. "They offered me food." In unison, the squirrels said, "Us, too!" The mice said, "Actual strawberries!" But the turtle — who had the low, slow, sad voice you'd probably expect him to have — said, "They told *me* I could have the use of their library."

Max sheathed his stick-sword in his belt loop and said, "This place stinks."

The ferret cleared her throat.

Max held up his hands. "Oh. No. I meant the Underground Town," he said quickly. "It's just not a nice place."

The ferret sighed again. "We know. We'd all return home in a heartbeat. But we're tied up so tight that we can't even think about escaping."

This gave me an idea. "Do you know where the dungeon is?" I asked.

The ferret shook her head to the best of her ability. "Not me."

In unison, the squirrels said, "Nope."

The turtle said, "I was unaware that such a place existed."

But one of the mice said, "I was there once — the warden twisted an ankle and needed something to sit on."

"Great," I said, turning to the mouse. "Could you get us there?"

"I could, from the main hall," she replied.

Suddenly my idea didn't seem so good. "How are we going to get to the main hall?" I asked. "We're being guarded."

"You could always avail yourselves of the servant passages," the turtle said. "There are secret passages in the walls so that as they perform their chores, the servants don't disturb the elves. There's a door over there in the corner."

And then, just as suddenly, my idea didn't seem so bad.

"Okay, animals," I said. "If we set you free, will you show us how to get to the dungeon?"

"I think I speak for us all," the turtle began, "when I say that we would accept your offer with some alacrity, provided you discerned some method whereby you could extricate us from our fetters."

Max put his hands on his hips in disgust. "Oh, come on," he said.

"Uh, Max," Emma said, "I think he's saying they'll help us, as long as we can get them out of their ropes." She looked around. "But how are we going to do that? We don't have a knife or anything."

That part took us a while to figure out, but eventually one of the mice said, "Do what we do!" So we started chewing. (And I never want to gnaw a rope with my nose buried in mouse hair again.) Eventually we freed one mouse, who freed the other mice, who freed everyone else. When we were done, I stowed some rope in my backpack, just in case.

Once free, the turtle said, "Onward!" and inched toward the back corner of the room. He pressed a button near the floor, and a door-shaped section of the wall swung toward us. The ferret checked the hallway beyond, and then led us quietly forward. (Well, as quietly as three person-sized squirrels, three mice, a turtle, and a ferret can walk on a wooden floor, which, with their claws, is really not that quiet.)

CHAPTER 9

THE PARK

We found ourselves in a hallway a lot like the hallway we'd taken to get to the room in the first place. It had stone floors, stone walls, and a stone ceiling. The only thing that wasn't stone was the wooden panel we had just walked through. Fortunately Emma had thought to bring a candle with her, because when we were all out and one of the squirrels closed the panel, it got very, very dark. It was so dark that even with the candle we could only see a few yards in either direction.

"Which way do we go?" I asked the ferret. I was whispering, because the hallway was so narrow and so dark.

The ferret shook her head and said, "Turtle, honey?"

"If I remember correctly from when I was a room service cart . . ." He paused here, I think because Max giggled. Somehow I managed not to laugh, but honestly, the idea of the turtle moving like molasses down the hall with food on his back struck me as funny, too. "If, as I say," the turtle continued, "I remember correctly, the servants' staircase lies in the northwest corner of the palace."

The ferret said gently, "Sweetheart, there's not a one of us who knows which way that is."

The turtle craned his neck, lifting his nose into the air and moving it around for a bit. Then he nodded back over his shell. "That way. Onward!" He then began scraping and scuttling in an attempt to perform a three- (or maybe six- or nineteen-) point turn in the narrow hallway.

Emma, Max, and I exchanged looks with the other animals, and then we all bent down, grabbed the turtle's shell, and started to carry him in the direction he had indicated. "Ah," he said, facing backward as we rushed him along, "a creative solution. I admire that. Onward!"

Soon enough we got to the servants' staircase. The turtle explained that two floors down we would reach a door to the main hall, and then one of the mice who knew about the dungeons would have to take over.

While we were resting, Max had a brilliant idea: we should get the glass table top off the turtle's back to make him lighter to carry. While Max and the animals worked, Emma and I posted ourselves in the corner of the building, where two corridors met, so we could watch for anyone coming.

It ended up taking some time, with Max and the other animals grunting, and the turtle saying things like, "You want to apply more leverage to the side," and, "I actually don't mind wearing this glass around. It's like having a skylight in my shell," and, "Please don't bother. I begin to fear that you will — ow! — do me an injury!"

The corner where Emma and I stood had a window, and so after a couple of minutes we found ourselves looking out at the Underground Town. We weren't that high up, but because the palace stood at the top of a hill and had the park all around it, we could see a long way.

I noticed that the tower lights — and I guessed the walls, too — went all around the city. The lights had gotten a lot dimmer, and the firefly lanterns provided most of the light along the streets, which I guessed meant it was nighttime. Still, though, I could make out what I figured must have been some of those broom-footed janitors sweeping the streets on the edge of the park. And just as I had begun to wonder about the janitor we had seen up close from the carriage — and started to think about how sad he had looked — Emma gasped, poked me, and pointed down at the ground just outside the palace.

At first I thought she was pointing at two Acro-Rats who were marching side-by-side along one of the paths in the park, but then Emma mouthed the word "kids," and I realized that the rats weren't exactly marching side-by-side. Between them was a line of half a dozen kids — little kids, about Lily's age — walking single file, carrying baskets. When they came up next to one of the wire trees, the rats crossed their spears in front of the kid at the head of the line, said something (I couldn't tell what, exactly, but it sounded like an order), shouted, "HAA!" and snapped to attention. The kids circled the tree, got down on their knees, and started taking things out of their baskets and sticking them into the ground.

Emma pressed her face up against the window and asked, "What are they doing?"

I couldn't tell. Partly because Emma was in the way now, and partly because with all those kids circling the tree, there wasn't enough light to see what they were up to from this distance. But then the Acro-Rats shouted, "HAA!" once more, and the kids stood up and formed a line. The rats led them to the next tree, and the whole thing started over again.

Now we could see what the kids had planted. As far as I could tell, they were flowers, which surprised me, because I didn't think you could just plop flowers into the ground and walk away like that.

Then I remembered the paper flowers planted around the wire trees, and I realized: these *kids* had put them there.

I was about to say something about this to Emma when three boys Lily's age came into view from around the side of the palace, accompanied by another Acro-Rat. The kids were carrying a tall step-ladder (it took all three of them to keep it moving), and when they got to the wire tree closest to us, they set it down (at one point the rat had to step in to keep it upright), and then, while two of them held the ladder steady, the third kid climbed it — and began hanging those metal leaves on the ends of the wire branches. It looked like the most boring job in the world, because after he put leaves on all the branches his kid-arms could reach, he had to climb down so the other two kids could move the ladder, and then climb up again.

Emma whispered, "This is crazy," at the glass and then pointed again. The park was filling up with kids and rats, and everywhere the kids were working. Putting in flowers. Replacing fallen leaves. Sweeping the paths. Raking the dirt between the trees.

All the kids were Lily's age, and none of them looked happy.

And then I remembered what Rhonda had said — that without the rats, nothing would get done that needed doing. I'd thought she meant that the rats did all the work. But now I got it: the rats made sure that *people* — *kids* — did all the work. But why did the elves need fake flowers and trees?

Just as I was thinking this, Emma leaned back from the window, her breath fading off the glass. "It just doesn't make any sense," she said.

What here does? I wondered. As far as I was concerned, we couldn't get Lily out of there fast enough.

Then we heard a *pop,* an "Ow!" and some muted cheering from the direction of the staircase. We looked over just in time to see Max leaning the turtle's glass tabletop against the wall.

Max hissed at us, "Guys, we're ready!"

Emma and I hurried over, and we all began to make our way down. It was a little awkward — it was a spiral staircase inside a square stairwell, and when we turned the corners, we had to carry the turtle on his side, which made him hard to hold. But eventually we made it down to the main hall. The mouse who knew the way guided us past the entrance (where the Acro-Rats were asleep, thank goodness), past the door to the now empty banquet hall, and on to a small side door, which was the door to the dungeons.

"Thanks, guys," I said as I held out my hand to the ferret. "I hope you get home safely."

She shook my hand and said, "Oh, I'm not worried, darling." Then she shook hands with Emma and Max, said to the other animals, "Let's go," and headed for the main entrance.

Max exchanged a complicated handshake with one of the squirrels — I don't know how they had time to learn it on the trip down — and then all the animals scuttled away down the hall after the ferret.

Except the turtle. He climbed up to a window, balanced himself on the sill, pulled in his head, legs, and tail, and fell out of sight.

We ran to the window. Below we saw that the other animals were already out and were helping to flip the turtle over because he had landed on his back.

Max leaned out. "Huh," he said. "I guess he did that to save them the hassle of carrying him out." And then, just as the ferret and the squirrels picked up the turtle and started running, Max looked up and shouted, "Hey! Mmm mmm mmm!"

Fortunately Emma had gotten a hand over his mouth before he challenged the rats in the park with his stick-sword, but I knew what had made Max mad.

"We saw the kids working, too," I said, and put my hand on his shoulder. "And all we can do is try to get Lily out of here."

Max looked out the window again. I realized that if it had been up to him, we would have declared war on the Acro-Rats and the Elf King right then and there and not stopped until every kid was free. But he sighed and turned toward the door to the dungeon. Emma and I went with him. This time we all wanted to lead the way.

CHAPTER 10

THE WRATH OF SHELFLIVER

The dungeon wasn't what I'd expected. The stairs were dungeon-like, stone steps spiraling down past stone walls, with iron rings set into them every few feet. But when we got to the bottom, we walked past a washer and a dryer. Then we walked past a room with a Ping-Pong table, a couple of beanbag chairs patched with duct tape, a beat-up video game console, and a television. Max shook his head. "Is this a dungeon or a basement?"

But from there it only took a few more feet to reach what *had* to be the dungeon. We came to a big room that still had vinyl tiles on the floors but also had five doors made of iron and wood set into a long stone wall. In each door was a window blocked by metal bars. Max said, "This is more like it," and pretty much skipped into the room.

"Great," I said. I was starting to feel a little nervous, and I just wanted to find Lily and get out of there. I called for her softly. No answer.

Emma looked as nervous as I felt. "Do you think she escaped?" she asked.

My first thought was, *She'd do that, wouldn't she?* Now that Emma mentioned it, I figured there was a good chance that Lily might be gone already. That's how things had started, after all — with Lily disappearing. But I wasn't ready to give up.

"She's here," I said. "I know it. And we're going to get her out." I heard a scuffling that had to be coming from behind one of the doors. I walked toward them. "Lily?"

"HAA!"

Suddenly four of the doors flew open, and the room filled with rats. Rats in tan uniforms. Rats in tall helmets. Rats with attitude.

Emma screamed, and behind me I heard Max shout, "Die, evil rat creatures!" Max launched himself at Sergeant Shelfliver, but he barely came up to the rat's waist. And so Shelfliver simply picked Max up, shook him a little, and half-pushed, half-threw him in my direction.

"SO!" Shelfliver hadn't gotten any less loud. "YOU DARE TO HELP A PRISONER ESCAPE?" He came over to me and leaned down to look me in the eye. "NOT SO EASY, IS IT? HA HA!"

When he said this, the other rats jumped in with another "HAA!" and Shelfliver looked around, annoyed. "CUT THAT OUT, YOU IDIOTS!" he screamed. "I WAS LAUGHING."

The look of shame on the faces of the other rats almost made me feel sorry for them.

That is, until Shelfliver wheeled around to face me again. "NOTHING GETS PAST ME," he shouted, "I HAVE SPIES." He snapped his fingers. (I learned then that rats don't snap their fingers like we do — they click their nails. It sounds equally loud. Just thought I'd mention it.) And when he snapped his fingers, there was some scuffling from the cell on the far end of the room . . . and Ear-with-Legs came out.

"HE HEARD ALL YOUR LITTLE PLANS WHEN YOU KIDS GOT SENT TO BED! HA HA!" There were a few shouts of "HAA!" in response, but Shelfliver ignored them. I ignored them, too, because I was making a mental note to never again discuss plans for a jailbreak on the other side of a door from an enormous walking ear. That was clearly a mistake.

Apparently Emma was mad, though. "You *told* on us?" she asked, looking at Ear-with-Legs.

He did one of his little bows in response.

"So basically," Emma said, "you're a snitch."

Ear-with-Legs stood up straight, as if he was offended. Then he stood on his left leg and tucked his right leg behind his — well, behind his ear. His foot brought something out, as if he had a pocket back there. I couldn't figure out what it was until he used his left toes to take the cap off a marker tied to the thing and began — *squeak, squeak* — to write. It was a whiteboard.

Everyone waited. Finally Ear-with-Legs capped the marker, balanced on his left foot again, and held the whiteboard up with his right foot.

It read: *OH, YEAH? YOUR STUPID*

Emma stamped her foot. "At least I can spell!" she shouted. "It's not *that* 'your.' It's the one with the apostrophe."

I think this threw Ear-with-Legs a little, because the ear kind of tilted to the side for a second. But then he wiggled from side to side, put the whiteboard down, rubbed away what he'd written with his foot, and started writing again. And this time it took him even longer to put down what he had to say, with his marker squeaking the entire time. When at last he put the cap back on the marker and held up the sign, I think I heard a couple of the rats give sighs of relief. (I might have sighed with relief, too, if it hadn't been for that whole trapped-in-the-dungeon thing.)

Now the whiteboard read: *I NO YOU ARE BUT WHAT AM I?*

"That doesn't even make sense!" Emma sounded more confused than mad. I think she realized she wasn't exactly arguing with her intellectual equal. Ear-with-Legs, however, wasn't through. He had uncapped his marker again — but he didn't start writing right away, as if he was thinking of a particularly biting response.

Shelfliver huffed and said, "GET ON WITH IT!"

Ear-with-Legs began writing — and squeaking. Finally he capped the marker and held up the whiteboard once more.

I'M RUBBER AND YOUR GLUE . . .

Ear-with-Legs flashed this triumphantly around the room, and then set the whiteboard down, ready to squeak his way through the second half of what he had to say.

Several of the rats groaned, and Shelfliver looked like his eyes were about to pop out of his face. "WE'RE THROUGH HERE," he shouted. "THROW THEM IN THE MIDDLE CELL."

Rats grabbed me and Max and Emma and hustled us toward the middle door.

"AND DON'T LET THEM OUT UNTIL THEY'VE WEIRDED SO FAR THAT THEY CAN'T GO HOME AGAIN. HA HA!" Shelfliver must have been laughing, because when one of the other rats said, "HAA!" in response, he glared at him until the poor rat fainted.

The rats threw Max, Emma, and me into the cell, and then slammed the door behind us. I shouted through the bars, "I just want to get my sister out of here. What's wrong with that?"

Shelfliver, who had turned to go, spun back to face me. "YOUR SISTER IS A CRIMINAL! LETTING HER ESCAPE WOULD LEAD TO CHAOS!"

I almost shouted back, *Why? Because if Lily got away, all the other kids might, too?* But I didn't — mostly because as soon as I thought to say that, I realized it was the truth. We couldn't be the only kids who wanted out, and Shelfliver knew it. So I just stood there, my hands gripping the bars, as the rats and Ear-with-Legs headed for the stairs. What else could I do? We were trapped.

And we still hadn't found Lily.

CHAPTER 11

UNDER THE WARDEN'S THUMB

Just when I was feeling the most hopeless, something good happened.

The narrow cell they had thrown us into stretched back a long way from the door. Folding cots stood on each side, leaving an aisle down the middle. A small table stood near the door and a single cot stood at the back wall. There was something on that cot — I thought it was a bundle of blankets, but because the only light came through the door, I couldn't tell. So I was startled and — honestly — a little frightened when the bundle started to move. I mean, it could have been someone weirded to look like blankets, I guess, or a hamster or some other animal tied down to serve as a cot, but in that split second I couldn't help wondering if a dungeon cell wasn't the most likely place for us to run into something really dangerous.

But then the bundle spoke.

"Isaac?" it whispered.

"Lily?" I squinted into the gloom.

"Isaac!" Lily threw off her blankets, rushed out of the shadows, and threw herself on me. For several minutes, she did nothing but cry and cling to me and cry some more. Emma helped by patting her on the back; Max *didn't* help by banging on the door with his stick-sword. When she finally calmed down, she told us her story. We already knew some of it, but her version made it sound as though she had just wanted to *look* at the Elf King's crown.

"And I lost mine," she said, "so how was I supposed to know that one belonged to him? It could have been mine."

I thought about lecturing Lily on manners and how you're supposed to behave around kings, but I figured she had been through enough (and anyway, I don't know much about how to behave around kings either). I also thought about digging her crown out of my backpack, but if *asking* the king about his crown had caused so much trouble, having her parade around in an imitation one seemed like a bad idea.

Anyway, Lily moved on. "Why did it take you so long to find me?" she asked.

I was about to explain the whole time moving differently thing when I noticed something strange about Lily's hair. I asked her to step closer to the door so I could see better, and then, not really sure if I wanted to know the answer, I asked, "How long would you say you've been here, Lily?"

"About a week," she said. "It took you guys *forever.*"

Only a week? No way, I thought. I mean, Acro had said a week, Rhonda had said a week, but I didn't want to believe it. Because when Lily stepped into the light of the doorway, it was obvious . . . the last two inches of each and every hair on her head had turned a bright ElfSelf pink. Only a week, and Lily had already started weirding.

"Oh, man," said Emma.

"We have got to get out of here," said Max.

"What?" Lily turned around to look into each of our faces. "What are you staring at?"

I was about to tell her when Emma jumped in. "You look like you've gotten taller since you came here."

"Really?" Lily asked as she turned to me. I nodded and forced a smile, because I realized Emma was right. There was no point telling Lily that she had started weirding, at least not until the rest of us started weirding, too. But how long would that be?

"What's that?" Emma asked. She went to the door. From out in the hall, we could hear a bell ringing.

"Oh, that?" Lily made a face. "It's just Opie. Probably with dinner."

Max joined Emma at the door, stick-sword ready. "It's the middle of the night," he said.

Lily shrugged. "Opie's crazy."

The bell got louder. I went to the door, too. I didn't mind the idea of food just then.

Finally the slow-moving figure of a bent old man came through the door, swinging a bell with one hand and balancing a tray waiter-style on the fingertips of his other hand. When he saw us at the window, he smiled. It wasn't until then that I noticed something funny about his face. It took me a minute and it took him coming closer, still smiling, before I figured it out. The man had a *thumb* — a big one, almost the length of my entire hand — growing out of the tip of his nose.

"Hel-lo!" He grinned like a maniac, and that, combined with the fact that his nose-thumb did a little wave at the same time, made it difficult to reply.

"Hello, Opie," Lily said, sounding bored.

"How is my little darling this evening?" Opie asked.

"It's the middle of the night," Lily replied.

"There's been a lot of excitement. New prisoners! Unavoidable delays." Opie swung the tray down. I was relieved to see that it held a plate of grilled cheese sandwiches, some carrot sticks, and apple juice in a pitcher.

"Stand back now," Opie said. "I'm going to open the door."

We did as he said. He brought in the tray, put it down, went out, and locked the door again. And then he stood at the window for a moment, considering us, while his thumb scratched at one of his enormous bushy eyebrows. We all looked back at him until finally he smiled.

"Escapees, eh?" he asked. His nose-thumb, having finished scratching, apparently decided it needed to smooth his eyebrow a little. So the thumb swiveled down toward Opie's mouth, where his tongue licked the tip, and then swung back up and went to work. Emma let out a whimper of disgust.

"Weirding isn't really something you have to run from," Opie said. "The little girl there will slip into elfishness as pretty as you please. The younger you are, the easier a time you have of it. She'll have the ears in no time. And for the rest of you, weirding isn't so bad. Some of us come to appreciate it. Look at me: in my job, it's a blessing to have a nose that can scratch itself." As he spoke, the thumb did exactly as he described — it scratched the side of his nose.

"And pick itself," Max sang out, laughing.

Opie cupped a hand to his ear. "What's that you say?"

Max couldn't answer, because once more Emma had put her hand over his mouth. But just then the thumb did a sort of pirouette, bent down toward

Opie's left nostril, and followed Max's suggestion. Emma put her hand over her mouth now, stifling a little scream.

"What?" Opie asked. He seemed genuinely puzzled, but I didn't say anything. I didn't see how it was my job to teach Opie manners. And then I wondered: what if his nose wasn't a part of him? What if it was really some other weirded person riding around on his upper lip? Even in that case, I decided, it wasn't my job to teach *anyone* manners. I just wanted to get us home.

"Isn't there any way we can get out of here?" I asked.

Opie blinked at me. His thumb relaxed, hanging down in front of his mouth. My question must have surprised him.

"Didn't you hear what I just said?" he replied. "Weirding is nothing to be worried about." He wrinkled his eyebrows for a moment, scratching his head, but then his nose-thumb shot out straight, and he snapped his fingers. "I know! Riddles. We can pass the time with riddles. Eh? Every time I bring you food, I'll ask you one. And then you ask me one. We'll make it interesting. If you can answer one of mine and I can't answer one of yours, then I'll let you go. How does that sound?"

Lily was right. Opie was crazy. But I didn't see how we had anything to lose from this proposition, so I said yes.

Opie jumped up and down, giggling. "Excellent! Excellent!" His nose-thumb gave a thumbs-up sign. And then, doing a little jig, he said, "Let's start! Let's start!" Then he gave his body a shake, took a deep breath, held himself up as straight as his bent skeleton would allow, and said, "I'll go first."

And so, one hand held forward with the index finger pointing up, one hand resting its fingertips on his chest, and his nose-thumb waving all around in crazy patterns as if it was too excited for Opie to control it, he started:

My peasants crawl with food in their jaws.
My soldiers defend and keep the laws.
My queen has babies without pause.
And if a queenling desires a throne,
She'll start a kingdom of her own.
What am I?

Then he stopped and looked around.

None of us said anything for a minute. I wasn't sure Opie had even asked us a riddle. Emma's eyes were wide and her mouth was open, as if she felt the same way. Lily just looked bored. Only Max looked interested. He was rubbing his chin as if he was thinking really, really hard.

Finally Opie cleared his throat. "Any guesses?" he asked.

Emma and I shook our heads. Max rubbed his chin a few more times and then shrugged. "A king?"

I was impressed that Max had even come up with a possible answer.

But Opie clenched his teeth and drew in a breath as if he felt sorry for us. "Oh, no. Sadly, no. The answer is actually in the first line, or part of it." He held himself up again with his hands in their dramatic poses, and said, "It's an ant colony!" Then he giggled and slumped again.

Apparently he didn't notice Emma mouthing the words "ant colony?" at Max and me, and us shrugging in response.

"Now it's your turn. Ask me one," Opie said excitedly.

Since Max had come up with an answer, Emma and I waited for him to come up with a riddle, too. But he shook his head, so Emma spoke up. "I think I've got one."

"Excellent." Opie leaned in close to the bars, his hand cupping his ear. "Ask away."

Emma looked at Max and me with a half-smile and a shrug, as if to say *I'm sorry, but this is the best I can do on short notice.* "What has four wheels and flies?" she asked.

Opie leaned back. His nose-thumb tapped his lips, which he had twisted to one side. "Oh, dear," he said, sounding a little embarrassed. "I do believe that's a garbage truck."

Emma shrugged. I wasn't that upset about Opie guessing correctly, since we hadn't had time to think of anything better. But Opie seemed disappointed that we had come up with such an easy riddle. He took his tray and left the room, calling over his shoulder, "Better eat up! Lights out in ten minutes."

Max, Emma, and I were starving, so we went ahead and ate the sandwiches. And even though I knew we should be coming up with riddles, we felt exhausted, so we decided to sleep on it and hope we'd come up with something in the morning. I have to say, though, that as much as I tried to remember riddles I had heard or read, it was hard to come up with any. I couldn't stop thinking about Lily's hair, or Opie's nose, or Rhonda's bottom. My best guess was that we'd only been there several hours now, but if we stayed overnight, how long would it be before we started to weird?

CHAPTER 12

MAX SAVES THE DAY

"Wake up! Time to eat!"

I didn't know what was going on — I felt like I had just gotten to sleep — but I sat up like a shot and felt my ears. It wasn't that I thought they might get pointy overnight — I just didn't want them taking over my body, like Ear-with-Legs. Once I was sure they were normal, I got up off my cot and went to the door. The lights were on, and the bell was ringing. In a moment, Opie appeared. He was carrying another tray of food, and he was grinning once more.

He shouted, "Wakey, wakey, chocolate cakey!" Farther back in the cell I could hear Emma and Max groaning and a little whimper I assumed came from Lily.

I rubbed my eyes and asked, "Is it morning?"

"Morning? Why would it be morning? I've just got more food for you," Opie said. Then he gasped as if he had just realized something very important. "More food? That means more riddles!"

That's when I understood what was going on. Opie came to the door and swung his tray down. On it, as promised, sat a chocolate cake plus some plates, some cups, and a pitcher of milk.

As Opie unlocked the door, we looked at each other. We had planned to sleep on the riddles we would ask and talk about it in the morning, but we hadn't gotten much sleep, and it sure as heck wasn't morning. It must have been only a couple of hours later, if that.

But Opie didn't seem to care. He put the cake down on the table, took all the leftover dishes from dinner away, and left the cell again. "Now I'll start, if you're ready," he said.

I hate to say it, but even with so much riding on guessing Opie's riddle, I couldn't get myself to wake up.

I just sat there, staring at the cake Opie had brought, while he took up his pose again and gave us another riddle.

I can take a deep breath and rise from the ground
Until a string grabs my tail and pulls me back down.
But my cousin can travel the world around.
She's swallowed a dragon whose fiery coughs
Make her head swell and send her aloft.

He leaned close enough to the door for his nose-thumb to grab the bars, and the corners of his mouth dug deep into the wrinkles on either side as he grinned. "What on earth could I be talking about?" he asked happily.

Neither Max nor Emma seemed ready with an answer, so I played for time. "Could you say it again?"

Opie struck his pose and said the words again. But they were more confusing the second time around. Pictures of dragons and people with swelling heads filled my mind.

Opie rubbed his hands together excitedly and said, "Answer, answer, let's have an answer."

"Fine," I said, pulling out an idea at random. "A cloud."

Opie's grin vanished, replaced with an insincere sympathetic expression. "Oh, what a shame. No. It's a balloon."

A balloon. Now I got the dragon thing — it was a party balloon talking about a hot-air balloon. Great. Because that happens all the time in real life.

"Your turn!" Opie's grin was back, and we hadn't come up with any riddles.

I looked at Emma and Max, and I even looked at Lily (who stuck her tongue out at Opie). But they had nothing, so I said the first thing that came to mind. "Where does an elephant keep his luggage?"

Opie slumped. I think he expected more from us. "Dear me," he mumbled. "In his trunk."

I slumped, too, thinking, *We're never going to get out of here.*

Opie walked away from the door, saying again, "Eat up."

We all looked at the cake and decided we'd rather get some sleep.

* * *

Ding, ding, ding, ding.

That bell again. The lights again.

I heard Emma groan from her cot.

I heard Lily mutter, "If we ever get out of here, I'm going to kill him."

And I heard Max say, "No, that won't work."

I sat up and looked over at Max. "What won't work?" I asked.

Max was sitting on his cot, his back to the wall. It looked like he had been there a long time. He seemed surprised that I had said anything. He said, "What?" and then, "Oh, nothing."

I might have asked again, except that at this point we heard Opie's creaky voice coming from the hall. "Wakey, wakey! Rice and hakey!"

Judging by how I felt, it seemed like we'd gotten even less sleep this time. But Opie was as cheerful as ever. He even did a little twirl as he came in with his bell and tray. It was only then that I realized we still didn't have a riddle to ask. And it struck me: was that Opie's plan? To keep us sleepy and confused so we couldn't stump him or guess his riddles?

By now Opie had come into the cell, and whatever he had on his tray made me wish I was back in the room with the ferret. It was some sort of fish on a pile of rice with red sauce poured over it. It did *not* look or smell appetizing, so, thinking fast, I snatched the cake off the table before he could take it away.

Opie didn't seem to notice. "Now," he said, once he had locked the door on us again, "are you ready for —" he did a little jig, and on his face his nose-thumb did its own little dance "— riddles?"

Through gritted teeth, I said, "Sure. Go ahead."

"Excellent! Excellent!" He danced a little more, his dress shoes clicking on the vinyl. And then, abruptly, he stopped and struck his pose — though of course, in his excitement, his nose-thumb continued to wave around.

I've got four brothers who are bigger than me.
They huddle together, but I stand free.
And when I'm not around, they tremble and trip,
And stumble and fumble and can't get a grip.

After he finished, Opie smiled a grin so wide and toothy it was like his face had unzipped itself in the middle. For a second I thought that unless his nose-thumb reached out and grabbed his chin his head was going to fall backward off his jaw. But then I thought about the riddle. *Stumble — fumble — grip?* That was a clue, wasn't it? I looked at the others. Emma was rubbing her eyes again; Lily was still stretched out on her cot, and might have gone back to sleep; Max was sitting with his back to the wall, eyes scrunched tight, his lips moving.

"Answer, answer!" Opie shouted.

"Give us a minute," I said.

Four brothers, I thought. *No, five.* Because there was the person talking, too. *Five brothers. Fumble. Grip.*

And suddenly I had it. I couldn't decide if Opie was getting cocky or if he just hadn't realized that the answer would be right in front of us.

"It's a thumb!" I shouted.

"What?" Opie asked. He stared at me, his nose-thumb scratching an eyebrow. "What did you say?"

"It's a thumb. A thumb!" Now it was my turn to jump up and down. I couldn't help it. We had answered one of Opie's riddles, and so all we had to do was . . . come up with one. Just like that, all the joy and triumph sank right out of me. We still didn't have a riddle of our own.

Opie knew it, too. He waved a hand in the air as if he didn't care (though I noticed that his thumb seemed to be moving around in nervous circles). "Well, that's how it goes sometimes. Now — let's hear yours."

Silence.

I looked at Max. He was still on his cot, eyes closed, talking to himself.

I looked at Emma. She shook her head.

Lily? Definitely asleep.

I racked my brain trying to come up with a riddle, and I had taken a breath and was just about to ask Opie, *What's black and white and red all over?* when Max came out of his trance.

"I've got one," he said.

Opie yawned, stretching his arms and his nose-thumb. "Let's hear it, then."

I figured I knew all the same riddles Max did. I didn't have much confidence that he'd come up with something that would stump Opie — I was just glad I wasn't going to have to ask one. But Max seemed to think he had something. He got off the cot and struck the same pose Opie had, finger in the air, hand on his chest. (I have to say that when Max did it, it actually looked kind of impressive.) Then he started.

I made me a pool out of butter and clay,
Filled it with oranges I found on the ground,
Let it bake in the heat of a cool fall day.
Then I broke my pool up to put it away,
And it dove into me with barely a sound.

Emma and I looked at each other, and then at Max. "What?" he asked, grinning. That's when I realized my mouth was hanging open.

"That was awesome, Max," Emma was smiling for the first time since we'd gotten into the furnace room. But you know who wasn't smiling? Opie. He had his arms crossed, with one hand stroking his chin. His nose-thumb kept thumping on his forehead as if it was trying to knock something loose in his brain. I thought about nagging him for an answer, but I was too busy enjoying the moment.

Finally, though, Emma must have realized that we needed to get going. "Opie?" She sounded sympathetic, but Opie growled at her. Literally growled, like a dog.

"Come on," I said. "Answer, answer!" Opie had said that to *us,* but apparently he wasn't ready to hear it himself.

"Stop that!" He slammed his fist against the bars. "Stop it, or you'll never get out."

I felt as if someone had poured ice water along my neck and shoulders. "But you said you'd let us out if we stumped you."

"Didn't say when, did I?" Opie turned and began to walk away.

I couldn't believe this was happening. *We won*, I thought. *Opie should be letting us out.* And if Lily was any indication, any moment now we would start to weird.

"You can't do this!" I yelled. Opie had reached the door out of the dungeon. He paused for a second and then kept walking.

Emma came up next to me at the bars. "You know what?" she said. "If you walk away right now, we'll never tell you the answer. And we'll keep coming up with riddles you can't guess, and we'll never tell you those answers either."

Now Opie came to a full stop, and I gestured at Emma to keep talking.

"Even when we've got purple hair and wings and pointy ears and are eating up at that high table thing, we will come down here and stump you until your head explodes!" Opie didn't move. So Emma took a deep breath, and in her best bossy voice, she jumped into the finale. "So you'd better come over here and open up this door, or else pretty soon you're going to wish you never locked us up in the first place!" (This, plus that fight with Ear-with-Legs, was showing me a whole new side of Emma.)

Opie's shoulders sagged. He turned around, walked back up the hall, and came to our door. "All right, then," he said. "What's the answer?"

Max laughed. "Nice try," he said, "but not until you open that door."

And so Opie did as he was told. And in a couple of minutes it was over. For the sake of appearances, we tied up Opie with the rope I took from the bedroom. We couldn't figure out what to do about his mouth until Max snapped his fingers, ran out of the room, and returned with some duct tape from one of the beanbag chairs. I woke Lily, who didn't even blink, really, at the fact that we had managed to escape. Then we ate some of the chocolate cake, took the keys, closed the cell door, locked it, and headed out of there.

Just as we were leaving the dungeon, we heard Opie in the cell. *"Mmmf! Mmmf mmmf mmmf MMMF mmmf?"*

"Oh, right," Max said. He shouted in Opie's direction, "It was pumpkin pie!"

We headed for the stairs.

CHAPTER 13

RUNNING FOR THE DOCKS

As it happened, we hadn't gotten more than about five steps up from the basement when we heard, "Escape! Escape! The prisoners are escaping!"

It made me kind of angry that Opie was already shouting for help. But Max shrugged and said, "That's what happens when you use old duct tape to silence a guy with a thumb on the end of his nose."

We all took about two seconds to reflect on the truth of that statement and then started running up the stairs again. Opie continued to shout from the basement, and I thought I heard sounds in the palace above us, but honestly — even though I was terrified of getting caught again, it was exciting running up those stairs. It was *fun,* even. And it continued to be fun as we ran up into the main hall, around to the front entrance, and through the pair of Acro-Rats who stood guard there.

They shouted, "HALT!" as we approached, but I shouted, "HAA!" back at them, and they snapped to attention just in time for us to run past.

At the foot of the steps, we found a carriage with a bunch of frogs standing around it. I ran up to them and asked, "Can you take us to entrance nineteen?"

I think the frogs might have been surprised by the question — or else their eyes were simply wide and surprised-looking already, since they were frogs. One of them said, in a deep, croaky voice, "Are you the king of the Underground Town, or the queen, or one of their duly appointed representatives?"

I shook my head.

"Sorry," the frog croaked. "Not in our contract."

By this time, bells were ringing in the palace, and I was starting to get nervous. "But you hate the elves," I said, crouching down to be at the frog's eye level. "And we're escaping from the Elf King. Don't you want to help us?"

The frog looked around at his friends. There was a chorus of negative responses.

"No."

"Not really."

"You must be joking."

The frog turned back to face me. "No, sorry," he said. "At the present time we are out of service. But thanks for the offer."

I was ready to beg, but then Emma said, "Isaac —" and pointed up the steps. About half a dozen Acro-Rats stood at the palace door, and as we watched them, they spotted us, leveled their spears, and charged.

"Okay, then," I said. "We're going on foot." We started running.

By the time we made it out of the park and into the town, bells were ringing all around us. I looked back and saw that the rats who had first chased us were still on our trail — and that an even bigger group of rats was coming through the park behind them. At this point, the adventure stopped being fun and started being completely terrifying.

It didn't help that as we started through the town, we began to encounter the people, or things, or whatever they were, who lived there, and that included a ton of firefly ladies. I guess they were changing shifts, because a lot of them were climbing up and down lampposts. Plus on every block you could see a few of them standing on the sidewalk in an unhappy-looking group. Max ended up barreling through one of these groups, knocking one firefly about ten feet down the road. He slowed down to see if she was okay and was instantly surrounded by a swarm of angry firefly ladies. He only got away because Emma waded into the crowd and dragged him out.

"Stay in the street!" I shouted.

Emma and Max started running along the cobblestones. Even there they had trouble. To go fifty yards, they had to dodge two people with donkey heads, one guy with the head of a moose, and one other person who was apparently made out of those long balloons they make swords and stuff out of at carnivals and birthday parties. (At first that guy looked like he was going to try to stop them, but Max waved his stick, and the guy went *squag, squag* out of the way, saying, "Don't puncture me! Don't puncture me!")

Why was I so far behind them? One word: *Lily*. I don't know if she was trying to make trouble or if she really was running as fast as her little legs could take her, but she kept slowing me down. We were about three-quarters of the way to entrance nineteen — I could see the tower ahead of us — when Lily tripped and fell. When I stopped to pick her up, she began crying.

"*Come on*," I said. The main group of rats was about a hundred yards behind us now, and they were gaining fast.

"Isaac, I'm sorry," she wailed, unable to stop crying.

"Lily," I said, "we don't have time for you to apologize now!"

She started crying harder. "Then I'm sorry I apologized!"

I slapped myself on the forehead. Then I thought of something. Did I have time for this? No. But I dug Lily's ElfSelf crown out of my backpack and handed it to her. "Take it," I said. "We've rescued you, so I guess you're officially a princess now."

But Lily kept crying. She said, "I don't feel like a princess."

I fished desperately around in my backpack until I found her ElfSelf doll. Now that Lily knew what real elves were like, I didn't think it would work, but it was worth a shot.

I handed her the doll, and to my surprise Lily stopped crying instantly. So that was good. But then she insisted on hugging me.

I pried myself away. "Okay, okay," I said. "But that's enough. We have to get out of here!"

The rats were maybe fifty yards away. But just as I had hoped, cheering Lily up made her run faster. As for myself, as I ran through the gateway, under the tower, and onto the boardwalk, I had a crazy thought that maybe the Olympic Track Team should hire some Acro-Rats to help them train. I know I had never run faster in my life.

CHAPTER 14

MY LAST STAND

By the time I got out on the boardwalk, Max and Emma had run all the way to the end of the dock, heading for the boat we had come in on. I had just enough time to wonder if this was a good idea when I heard someone scream, "*Aaaaaah!*" and heard a splash. Lily and I sprinted to the end of the dock, and I saw a pair of hands flailing around in the lake. I looked at Max. He shrugged, said, "Hans got in the way," and then reached to help Lily into the boat.

Now it was my turn to get in, but just as I did so, I realized three things. First, we were still tied up to the dock. Second, the pole for the boat was stuck in a holder on the dock. And third, I could hear the echoing patter of rats' feet coming through the gateway.

They're almost here, I thought, and as I jumped out to untie the boat, I did some quick thinking. As soon as they got to the boats, the rats would come after us. We might not even get to the rushes before they caught us. And if we went back to the dungeon, we might never get out until we had turned into fireflies or pretzels or balloon animals. *And it would all be my fault*, I thought. I had led everybody to the Underground. I had lost the jewel gem. If we didn't get out, it would all be on me.

I can't let that happen, I told myself. As soon as I undid the rope, I grabbed the pole from its holder, jammed one end against the side of the boat, and pushed it with all my might in the direction of the outgoing rushes. The boat shot forward, and, pole in hand, I started running back up the dock.

Emma shouted, "What are you doing?"

"Helping you get away!" I called. As I ran, I saw the first rats coming out of the gateway. I ran faster.

"What about you?" Emma cried.

"Don't worry about me!"

The rats were almost onto the dock now. I lowered the pole and charged at the one in the lead. He went, "Oof!" and fell backward, knocking down several others as he fell. I swung the pole around and knocked the next one over, and then advanced, swinging at another. He backed off. In seconds, all the other rats had retreated back under the tower.

I took a moment to be proud of my plan. My boat pole was longer than their spears and way longer than their swords. If they kept coming at me one at a time, I could hold them off as long as I had strength in my arms.

"Isaac! Come back now! You could swim!" That was Emma.

It was tempting. But I couldn't do it. Not until my friends and my little sister had reached the rushes and had enough of a head start to get to the other side. "Don't worry about me!" I called again. (*You* try thinking of one-liners while you're fighting off a horde of supersized rats.)

The rats pushed one of their comrades out of the gate. After a couple of resentful looks back at the other rats, he came forward, spear level. Then, to my complete surprise, he started to run. I backed up, but I wasn't sure where the boardwalk ended, and when I looked under my feet to check, I tripped and ended up falling to my knees. *Where's that rat? How am I going to fight him off?* Those were the only thoughts I had time for as I felt the boardwalk shake under his running feet.

He was right over me, spear at the ready — when something hit him on the head, and he stopped, staggered around, and fell over into one of the boats. He was out cold.

I heard cheering and realized the rock had come from the boat, where Max, Emma, and Lily were launching Acro's ballast.

I picked myself up, turned to them, and shouted, "Way to go!"

Lily shouted, "Isaac, come on!" But at the same time, Max shouted, "Look out!"

I swung back just in time to knock another running rat off the boardwalk and into the water. Then another came, but when a rock from the boat landed on his foot, he stopped just long enough for me to knock him down. There was a pause in the attacks then, and I ventured a look back at the boat. It was moving a little faster now than before, caught, I hoped, in an outbound current that started before you got to the rushes. *Just another minute,* I thought, *and they'll be free.*

Then I heard something I didn't want to hear ever again — the voice of Sergeant Shelfliver. "WHY AREN'T YOU ON THE DOCK?"

"HE'S HOLDING US OFF, SIR!" one of the rats replied.

There Shelfliver was, standing in the gateway. Frowning at me, he drew his sword.

"THEN ATTACK HIM ALL AT ONCE, IDIOTS!" Shelfliver cried. "HAA!"

Next came a couple seconds of silence as Shelfliver glared at the others. Then one of the rats — I couldn't see who — said, "I'm sorry, sir, but were you laughing?"

"I'M CALLING YOU TO ATTENTION! HAA!" An answering "HAA!" came from all the other rats as they stood at attention. They suddenly looked a lot more frightening than they had a second before.

Shelfliver pointed his sword in my direction. "TWO SQUADS, FORWARD MARCH. TWO SQUADS TO BOATS WHEN WE MAKE THE DOCK!" He marched toward me, sword out, and eight Acro-Rats formed two lines of four behind him, matching his pace.

I backed up a little. There was only enough room for two or three rats to walk side by side on the dock. If I could hold them there for a moment, it might be long enough for my friends to get away.

Shelfliver noticed what I was doing. He shouted, "HA HA!" — I was pretty sure he was laughing, but when the other rats answered with a deafening "HAA!" he didn't seem to mind — and said, "NOT MUCH FUN — IS IT, BOY? — FIGHTING A SWORD WITH A BOAT POLE?"

"What boat pole?" I asked. The rats were almost at the dock. I gripped the pole until my knuckles turned white. "This is a sword."

"HA HA!" Shelfliver laughed. All the other rats were pouring from the gate now, and their answering "HAA!" echoed across the water like thunder. "THAT'S NOT A SWORD."

"It is if I say it is!" I shouted.

From a distance behind me, I heard Max shout, "Isaac, you dufus! It's not a sword — it's a lance!"

More rocks fell into the water around me, and I realized that this was good news. It meant that my friends were out of range. The bad news? The rats were out of range, too.

And then I heard Lily shout, "What is that?"

I had only a split second to wonder what she was talking about before Shelfliver shouted, "CHARGE!" and bolted in my direction.

This is it, I thought.

I swung the pole, but Shelfliver blocked it with his sword and sent me spinning.

I lost my balance and started to fall.

But the fall seemed to last a long, long time.

And it was accompanied by a weird jerking sensation in my shoulders and stomach.

And somehow it involved me falling *away* from the dock instead of down to it.

And suddenly I realized that I wasn't falling, but flying — gliding in the direction of the wall and the tower. Gliding over the heads of a bunch of astonished rats, with something dark and flappy gliding above me.

"Whatever you do, don't let go of that pole." The dark flappy thing had a voice I vaguely recognized. I pondered it for all of the three seconds it took for us to get to the tower.

"Brace yourself," the voice said. And I'm glad he did. Because I barely had time to put out my legs when we hit the side of the tower — and I barely had time to tighten my grip on the pole before, with a grunt, the flappy thing jerked us about ten feet higher than where we had landed.

I looked up. I saw sweatpants. That plus the voice finally helped me figure out who had rescued me.

"Acro?"

A grunt. "Yep."

I looked down. We had to be about four stories above the boardwalk now, but still, with another jerk, the Acro-Bat took us higher.

"What are you doing?" I asked.

"I couldn't let so valiant a warrior go down alone," he said.

Another jerk, and we went up another ten feet.

"No," I said, as he jumped us up another ten feet. "I mean what are you *doing*?"

"Saving you. Hold onto the pole."

Suddenly there was another jerk, but instead of it ending with us higher up on the tower, it *didn't* end. I thought we were falling, and I screamed.

And when I saw that we *were* falling — that the water and the dock and a bunch of confused and angry rats were rising toward us with sickening speed — I screamed again.

And when I saw Sergeant Shelfliver shake his paw at us and shout, "YOU'LL PAY FOR THIS, BAT!" I screamed once more.

And when we sailed out past the end of the dock and over the water, I screamed for the fourth time.

And then, when we were about ten yards from the boat, and I thought we were going to land right on the ballast — well, I didn't scream then, but honestly? I'm pretty sure that's only because I passed out.

* * *

When I came to, Emma, Max, and Lily were standing over me.

"Hey! He's awake!" I think Emma said that, but I can't be sure.

I was still pretty out of it. It felt like every part of my body was collecting the scattered pieces of my stomach and putting them back together in my throat.

Max crouched beside me. "You okay?" he asked.

I nodded. I didn't feel up to talking just then. I decided to try sitting, and that actually went pretty well. Acro-Bat was standing in the back of the boat, poling us forward — and I remembered what had just happened.

"The rats!" I almost jumped up to look behind us, except that about three-quarters of me seemed to think that this would not be a good idea.

"Acro doesn't think they're going to follow us," Emma said as she knelt next to me. "He says they don't like to ride the rushes."

Max punched me in the shoulder and said, "So it was a good plan you had, except for the getting yourself left behind part."

"I would have missed you!" Emma said. She gave me a big long hug, and I realized how much I would have missed her, too.

Now Lily sat down next to me. She still had on her ElfSelf crown, and her hair was still pink, but she didn't seem frightened or sorry anymore. "And I was going to have to explain everything to Mom and Dad," she said. "Did you ever think about that?"

CHAPTER 15

GETTING OUT OF THERE

With Acro poling the whole way, it took a lot less time to go back than it had going over, which was good, because I was getting worried about time again. I mean we'd been in the Underground Town *overnight*, so surely some serious time had to have passed aboveground. And when we slowed down and Acro had to pole us around the rocks, I got even more worried.

But we did eventually reach the dock. Max jumped off and tied the boat up, and we all got out. Acro came with us, and we stood around for a moment.

Finally I said, "Thanks." (I had already thanked him on the boat, but I couldn't come up with anything else to say.)

"Don't mention it," Acro said. He took off his baseball cap, scratched his head, and then put the cap back on. As he did so, I noticed again that it had a crown embroidered on the front.

"What's going to happen to you now?" Emma asked him. "Are you in trouble?"

Acro shrugged his bat wings. "I should probably avoid the Underground Town for a while. I think I'll go back to my people."

"Your people?" Max scrunched up his face in confusion. "Aren't your people in the Underground Town?"

"No, just me," Acro said. "Almost all the Acro-Bats live in their own country, in another part of the Underground."

Acro cleared his throat as if he was a little embarrassed about something, then said, "I'm, um . . . well, I'm actually king there, if you want to know the truth."

King?

"Then why were you working for the elves?" Max asked. "Food?"

Acro just shook his head. "I had my reasons. Maybe I'll tell you some other time."

Now came a pause in the conversation. For my part, I was trying to remember — or maybe just imagine — what you were supposed to do when you met a king.

Weren't you supposed to kneel, or bow, or call him "Your Majesty" or something?

I was getting ready to bow when Max spoke up. "If you're a king, you could make me a knight!"

Acro-Bat cocked his head. "I think you're right about that," he said.

"Cool!" Max swept his stick-sword out of his belt loop and made a big show of handing it to Acro. Then he went down on one knee. "Make me a knight!"

Acro gave the slightest shrug, then used the stick to tap Max on each shoulder and the top of his head. "Arise, Sir Max."

Max shot up like a rocket. "Yes! Yes! Yes!" He did a little dance. "Woo-hoo!"

Acro looked questioningly at me and Emma.

I thought, *It would be cool to be an actual knight.* So I went down on one knee, too, and so did Emma, who must have been feeling the same way.

Acro did the tapping thing with the stick on me, then said, "Arise, Sir Isaac."

I stood up. Believe it or not, I felt *different* after that, as if something had changed in me.

I heard Acro say, "Arise, um, *Sir* Emma," and looked over. Judging by Emma's expression — her eyes had gone wide, and she had a faint smile on her face — she felt different, too.

Of course, this was when Lily spoke up. "Make me a princess!"

Acro blinked at her. "What?"

Lily sat down in front of him. "Make me a *princess.*"

"I'm new to this whole knighting thing, but I'm pretty sure I can't make someone a princess, only a knight," Acro explained.

"I want to be a princess!" Lily demanded.

"Lily —" I began. Trust my little sister to make things awkward.

Acro waved me off. "No, no. It's fine." He tapped Lily (she giggled when he did this) and said, "Arise, Princess Lily."

She stood up, looking pretty much as happy as Max, who was still jumping around and shouting.

Acro handed me the stick-sword. "See that he gets this back," he said, nodding toward Max. "And always remember that a sword can be anything you use to do the work of a knight."

I nodded in response, but I really wasn't sure what he meant.

"And now I should go, and so should you, in case the rats do decide to cross the lake," Acro said. He walked back down the dock to the boat.

We waved to him as he poled away — not back in the direction of the Underground Town, but along the lakeshore.

When he was about twenty feet away, Emma shouted, "Will we ever see you again?"

Acro thought about this for a moment. "So far," he called, "you're the only knights I have. So if I come up with any quests that need doing, I'll be in touch."

Max answered for all of us. "Great!" He added a little jump after he said this, and that pretty much answered for all of us, too.

Because his course along the shore took him out of the light instead of into it, Acro disappeared quickly into the darkness, but before he went out of sight, he stuck his pole in its holder, climbed to the top, and did a triple somersault and a full twist in the air before once more nailing the landing. He bowed, and we applauded, and then we turned to go.

As we were leaving the dock, though, a strange thing happened. Or I guess one *more* strange thing.

Emma said, "Huh," and bent down. When she came up, she was holding something small and made of red plastic.

Lily said, "My jewel gem!" and held out her hand.

Honestly? I wasn't all that thrilled to see it. It had started the whole thing, after all. I was glad, though, that Lily was finally going to get it back. But as Emma handed the jewel gem off to Lily, it slipped out of her fingers and rolled all the way along the length of the dock as if it was going downhill, *clicketit, clicketit, clicketit.* At the end of the dock, it seemed to jump up in the air, and then it landed *plop* in the water and was gone.

Emma just stared.

Max said, "Wow."

I looked at Lily, because I really expected her to start crying.

But Lily just said, "Whatever," and started for the passage that led back to Castle Elementary. We followed her.

* * *

There isn't much to tell after that. We got back to the furnace room pretty much right after we left, and after about thirty minutes, the door opened to reveal Old Man McTavish, two police officers, and Emma's mom. When she spotted us, Emma's mom shouted up the stairs, "They're down here!" In about ten seconds, the room was filled with my mom, Max's dad, Emma's mom, Mrs. Applebaum, and Mr. Williams, our principal. There was a little bit of "I was so worried." There was a brief moment of "Why was this door locked on both sides?" There were a couple minutes of "We could sue the school system." (Emma's mom is a lawyer.) Then we all went home.

On the way, Mom kept saying over and over how worried she had been. (And I guess she was worried, since she didn't notice Lily's hair until we got home.) But I tuned her out. I had a lot to think about. I wondered if any other kids from Castle Elementary had ever made it into the Underground. I wondered how Old Man McTavish could not know about it. I wondered if that explained why the furnace room door had a lock that needed a key on both sides. And I wondered when Acro would be getting in touch with us. I was sure, somehow, that it would be soon.

But as we drove through town, I also thought about how weird it was that the Underground was beneath my school. And it wasn't just under the school, or even just under the hill it sat on. It was everywhere. Under Bennettville, too under the First Bank of Bennettsville. Under the Bennettsville Historical Museum. Under Bennettsville Pizza, the Bennettsville Stop and Shop, and the Bennettsville Gas Station and Auto Emporium. Under my neighborhood. *Under my house*. Under my house, there was a town, and a lake, and a world full of creatures no one knew about.

You might think that knowing that all that was down there would make Bennettsville seem smaller, but it did just the opposite. Somehow thinking about the Underground made the world aboveground seem bigger and stranger. Bigger and stranger and a lot more fun.

It's a great place to be a knight, I thought.

ABOUT THE AUTHOR

Douglas Gibson and his wife and son live in lovely Asheville, North Carolina, along with a small dog named Spencer and a medium chicken named Juliet. When he isn't writing about books or designing them for other people, Douglas is usually hard at work writing books of his own.

ABOUT THE ILLUSTRATOR

Jez Tuya is a New Zealand–based freelance illustrator. With over five years of experience, Jez specializes in character design and children's illustration. He has also held gallery shows with Light Grey Art Lab in Minneapolis, Minnesota.

GLOSSARY

alacrity (uh-LAK-ri-tee) — a cheerful readiness or willingness to do something

ballast (BAL-uhst) — heavy material (like rocks, sand, or water) that is put on a ship to make it more stable and less likely to tip over

deserted (dih ZUR-tid) — completely empty of people

extricate (EK-stri-kayt) — to free someone or something from a dangerous or difficult situation

proposition (prop-uh-ZI-shuhn) — an offer for a person or a group of people to consider

sinister (SIN-uh-stur) — looking or seeming evil and threatening

standard operating procedure (STAN-derd OP-uh-rey-ting pruh-SEE-jer) — a phrase that means how something is normally done or handled

valiant (VAL-yuhnt) — showing great courage and bravery

For downloadable writing prompts and discussion questions, plus more cool books, visit CapstonePub.com.